ACCLAIM ►

C000043418

'Chris Kelso is intelligence, w page there is evidence of a great mind at work. Just when you're wondering if there are actually still writers out there who still feel and live their ideas out on the page, I come across a writer like Kelso, and suddenly the future feels a lot more optimistic. One calls to mind Burroughs, and Trocchi's more verbose offerings –whilst remaining uniquely himself, in a writer as young as he is, is a very encouraging sign: one of maturity that belies his youth. I look forward to reading more from him in the near future.'

► **Andrew Raymond Drennan, author of The Immaculate Heart**

'Chris Kelso sets his photonic crystal gun on KILL and takes no prisoners. My favorite era of science fiction was the 60s "New Wave" when the British magazine NEW WORLDS took front and centre, and there's a bit of NEW WORLDS here, kind of like Jerry Cornelius using the cut-up method in a bungalow in Glasgow, with a splash of Warren Ellis added for extra flavour. Kelso has a compelling voice. Somewhere Papa Burroughs is smiling.'

► **L.L. Soares, author of Life Rage and In Sickness**

'Chris Kelso's writing is like a punch to the gut that forces your face against the page. The way his gritty prose carries his imagination is like a bar fight between Bradbury and Bukowski, with the reader coming out on top. The worlds he drags us into are so damn ugly that you have to admire their beauty.'

► **Chris Boyle of BizarroCast**

'Whether he's writing about a fictionalized William Burroughs, Time Detectives, or Aliens Chris Kelso aims at the interstices or the Interzones because he understands that these are the people and spaces that define modern life – Kelso is also always funny and twisted.'

► **Douglas Lain**

'Choke down a handful of magic mushrooms and hop inside a rocket ship trip to futuristic settings filled with pop culture, strange creatures and all manner of sexual deviance.'

► **Richard Thomas, author of** Transubstantiate

THE

DISSOLVING

ZINC THEATRE

▸ The Dissolving Zinc Theatre

▸ Villipede Publications

PO Box 3643

Idaho Falls, ID 83403

villipede.com

Special discounts are available on quantity purchases. For details, contact the publisher at the address above.

Printed in the United States of America

ISBN-13: 978-0692428726

ISBN-10: 0692428720

« First Edition »

FOR LOUIE

Works by Chris Kelso ▸

Novellas

A Message from the Slave State

Moosejaw Frontier

Transmatic

Short Story Collections

Schadenfreude

Terence, Mephisto & Viscera Eyes

Novels

The Dissolving Zinc Theatre

The Black Dog Eats the City

Magazines (with Garrett Cook)

Imperial Youth Review issue 1

Imperial Youth Review issue 2

Comics

The New Animal Liberation Front

Anthologies

Caledonia Dreamin' – Strange Fiction of Scottish Descent (ed. With Hal Duncan)

Terror Scribes (ed. With Adam Lowe)

" I don't see any God up here. "

▸ *Soviet Cosmonaut Yuri Gagarin*

a decagonal of nails descending, scratching like tacks, tearin...

RAVINSKY

Helixes of blood that fo...

...shadow and sense of dread...

consuming

destroyed city of so...withing cardboard...the ruins beneath my feet...th

I had this dream where I was walking through the thrown ramparts of a

HERE

Blue is the colour of the sky-ay-ay

...good to be back.

peel off in great charred strips.

noisy, agitated fly.

The panpipe music swirls around his s...

MMENSETTER

half-aborted fetus

...one of the ser...-

Cemetery Ga...

ready a member of the Académie française and The Royal Academy of Belgium.

KNUCKLES TORN, RIVETTED

Sh

...stotle

autumn

CHRIS KELSO—OR THE ART OF DISSOLVING GENRES

Let's play upfront from the start: Chris Kelso's *The Dissolving Zinc Theater* is a masterpiece, a real "Modern Classic" in its own right. With this novel, Kelso is definitely opening new doors and showing new directions in fiction. The story is as complex as it is simple— without deflowering it, let's say that it revolves around a film in the making—or is it filmS in the making? We will actually never quite know—and the different characters—or is it persons, we will never quite know either, as some are more or less androids—hovering around it. It is a mix of intellectual discussions, bizarre sex scenes and, of course, terrifying violence. Imagine Fellini's *81/2* crisscrossed with *Naked Lunch* and you have something quite close to the feeling I had while reading it.

I have been following Kelso's work for a little while now, and enjoyed tremendously both his *Transmatic* and *The Black Dog Eats the City.* This young writer is not only a rising star of "Weird" fiction, but also someone, like Burroughs, Ballard, Moorcock or Lovecraft, who has managed to create a completely idiosyncratic world and style. Many authors like to mix genres, but Kelso's mix hovers above the rest because it is relevant. There is nothing to cut from the text, no fat, no unnecessary reference—the architecture is extremely finely tuned and solid, yet strangely delicate.

And then there are the drawings, the strange lines moving across the pages, the deleted sentences and paragraphs—nothing new here, of course, and yet there is something extremely refreshing in the re-use of this old gimmick, something I dare to say that has not been done before. Baudelaire said that modernity was surprise, and Kelso is radically modern by this standard. I am actually sure that the old French poet would have gracefully shared his opium pipe with him.

The Dissolving Zinc Theater is not an easy read, by any means, but it is a rewarding one for all those who love literature, and who are tired of "meaningless" works. There is deep meaning here, under the tongue-in-cheek humor and apparent chaos, I would even say an existentialist meaning, in the good old use of the term. A Surrealist Humanism (albeit a dark one, but we're still fucking up the rest of the world, no?), which does justice to the illuminating intuitions of Breton, Artaud and Daumal.

Yes, I love this book. I love it because, in my eyes, it is an important work that gives literature back its original purpose, linked with tragedy: catharsis. As you read it, you will be amazed, you will be terrified, you will be awed. And you will love it too, for all the wrong reasons, which are, of course, all the good reasons.

▸ *Seb Doubinsky*

I had that same dream . . . walking through the thrown ramparts of a destroyed city of soggy, wilting cardboard . . . the ruins beneath my feet . . . the awful, consuming shadow and sense of dread . . .

ONE

Intertitle: The Dissolving Zinc Theatre

(*Black screen*)

[The cold open, a slow dissolve . . . fading in of soft violin music, soaring then plunging, then soaring . . . image of a Baroque painting fills the perfect square of the television set—a naked woman breastfeeding a goat-legged man, cuddled together like hibernating rattle snakes. The camera zooms out from the painting until it is just a framed picture on the wall of a cottage. Pan across the room to a sad-faced elderly man with his head in his palms sitting at the dinner table. His elbows are scuffed and sandy; his fingernails are encrusted with thick clumps of dirt.

He knows we're watching. He is a riddle in nine syllables . . .

Sound of falling clapboard . . .

In an overwhelming self-awareness, the old man starts weeping behind the broad mask of his hands. The violin music gets louder, crystal glasses fracture but do not shatter, before a soprano voice starts projecting tragic librettos in Italian.

Unanimous expression of the seagulls' squawked siren. The old man is outside, sunk half deep in mud, trying to straighten a wilted barren tree. He curses to himself as the jagged branches poke at his face and break off around him. His world is rickety, splintered, unreal. Sky is the colour of sickly marrow behind thin vapour. The sea looks ready to rise beyond the sand pits and submerge everything beneath its surge. A Japanese flute starts tooting as the tree breaks in half, prat-falling the old man into the swathes of muck. He tries getting up but there is nothing to grasp but handfuls of wet dirt. In one last effort, the old man extends his reach to the strongest looking branch stemming from the tree's body. Under his weight it snaps and crumbles like any other rotted, brittle twig. He sinks into the dirt and lets it cover his face. The old man waits for what must've been a good couple of hours, lying perfectly supine, until the mud thins and he can push forth like a zombie breaking free from its grave.]

{ *A half-dead man with lacy, wart-thrown fingers raises the curtain. He tugs it with all his effort. His head is a mirror. You see, you see. All over his rotted body there's proof of blood and bad chow—a hessian of eczematic, rheumy flesh. A bib of sneezed out macaroni all the way down his chest, below—gut wound exposed, the caviar of vital organs spilling out over the verge. Complexion blenched, icicles dangling from septum . . .*

Slow murder in the key of C. There is blood and semen on the once expensive eiderdown. I provide a service. People these days do not want to feel—why should they? All feeling leads to is hurt and pain and loneliness. We've learned that much at least, surely? A burning sun orbits above mountains of hot excrement and steaming trash on a landfill, bringing new communities inside my brain to venture out to the wasted open space in search of recyclable material. If you can plug those senses that let in all the hurt, you can have some semblance of happiness, cos otherwise, you're just waiting to drop dead, you know? You know you're gonna die, we all do, you know that love doesn't ever prevail, everything ends. There ain't no point to anything . . . so why would you want to sit around all day THINKING about dying? What would be the point? You might as well kill yourself now, cos lemme tell ya, that ain't no way to live a life, buddy. My films stimulate the senses; make a drone of the sentient. I can mute the voice in the human head, the voice that sends rational thought swirling around your brain like a self-fulfilling virus . . . I'll

fill you with synthetic love, keep you believing in the make-
believe. Give you hope. This is not the generation for the
vulnerable or sensitive individual, you can't survive that
way, not anymore . . . }

[The sad music starts again . . .]

[Scene opens on an image of a tiny farmhouse potted
miles off in the distance. It belongs to the old man
(when we eventually cut to him sitting on an
upturned bucket the sad music begins on cue).

The old man is called Klopp.

While Klopp wipes muck from his skin and clothes, a
young boy cycles past who looks like a half-aborted
foetus. Klopp gives an expression that would suggest
he is pleased to see the boy. He calls over to him,
« *Come help me wash this filth away!* » The boy hops off
his bicycle and picks up the garden hose with such
smoothness and speed it's almost like one fluid
motion. Klopp removes his overalls and stands in a
starfish shape waiting for the freezing jet of water to
punch him clean. The boy twists the nozzle and, sure
enough, a hammer-fist of liquid blasts old Klopp

straight off his feet and up into a tree. The boy rushes over and looks into the maze of branches and leaves.]

Patrick Laughs, Polly Cries

I fall down the stairs and break my pinky toe. Patrick laughs. Polly cries.

I make a sandwich and catch my finger when cutting the bread into triangles. Patrick laughs. Polly cries.

I'm late for work, my boss fires me. Patrick laughs. Polly cries.

Every taxi I try to hail speeds right on past. Patrick laughs. Polly cries.

My girlfriend leaves me and takes my cat.

Patrick laughs. Polly cries.

(Camera face zooms in)

« Are you alright? » [yells the boy.]

« I'm . . . yes, I think so . . . »

« You really took off there! Like a kite or something,

WHOOSH! »

[The boy ceases his sunny disposition. There is a
pregnant pause. Someone holds up a cue card off-
shot. Klopp has a defeated expression.]

« It's probably best I'm up here out of the way. »

« What makes you say that? »

« Oh, no reason . . . »

« Go on, tell me! I'll tell you a secret! »

« Okay, you go first then. I'm too self-conscious to talk

about it all right now. »

« Promise you'll tell me? »

« Yes, yes . . . I . . . yes, I'll tell you, yes . . . »

« Well, alright then . . . »

[The boy squirms awkwardly. He scratches at a sore
behind his ear until it bleeds. This is ad-libbed.]

« The thing is, the thing is that . . . I don't like music. »

« That's it? »

« Well, yes! »

« Oh, my boy! Goodness, my boy . . . I . . . »

« So what's yours? »

« I shouldn't say. No—it's really quite humiliating! »

« You promised! »

« *Oi*, fine . . . »

« Come on then! »

« Okay, yes . . . just . . . okay . . . give me a minute, you
little rat! »

[Klopp untangles the varicose vines and twigs from

around his ankle and climbs down the trunk of the tree. A stream is loudly surging past with water so dirty you can barely see an inch beneath its surface. The boy is waiting with a face of pure relish and anticipation.]

« You don't like music, boy? Well I *can't escape music!* »

« What? »

« Sad music, in particular. I can't escape it. I wake up in the morning and these violins burst all around me. It's plagued me my whole life. »

« Well I don't hear anything right now. »

[The old man waits with his ear to the air.]

« You're right! »

« You old liar! »

« No, no, you see this has never happened before! »

« So why's it happening now? »

« I'm not sure. You say you hated music? Maybe you scared it all away. »

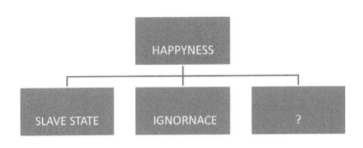

{ *People think I'm contributing to the retardation of society, well let me tell ya, I'm glad. People think too much in my opinion, that's why we're so fuckin' unhappy. Maybe it's time to switch off, for just a moment, huh, switch off? Destroy the ego they all say, but I'm a fuckin' writer, ego is my life! Plus all those assholes who go on journeys to find themselves, that'll cure them of their indomitable selfishness, so they think. Well Jesus, isn't that the most egotistical voyage imaginable? Trust me, I'm helping society. I was a sensitive guy once, oh yeah. I loved anything that was deep and meaningful, then I got my stupid heart handed to me on a plate and now I know better. Anyway, it doesn't matter . . .* }

[Klopp puts his arm around the boy and leads him into his home, away from a parade of slave-children. There's no sense in the young boy having to see the awful things that lie ahead in his future . . .]

■

(Chyron: **Hollywood, Celluloid Studios**)

[Klopp sits at the table, his face a portrait of inner peace, and beams at the boy. The camera cuts to the boy and stays on him for several minutes. Silence.]

« You mustn't ever leave my side . . . uh, mister . . . ? »

« Stanley. »

« Stanley, I will pay you six dollars to live with me on this farm. »

« I don't think I'll be able to do that, Mister Klopp, sir. »

« And why not? »

« ~~Well, my father wouldn't agree to it.~~ »

[The boy doesn't respond.]

[A stage-hand walks clumsily into the frame holding a boom-pole. A fierce voice yells out—]

" CUT! "

[The Director comes rushing onto the set. People can be heard gasping. The Director moves toward the stage-hand until there is barely a sliver of daylight between them. He draws a large samurai sword from his belt with a *SCHLUNK* and raises the thin blade above his head.]

" This picture is three hours long, *THREE-HOURS-LONG.* This is only the third scene from the end and you've ruined it—RUINED it! Now we must start again. Hand *OUT!* "

[The quivering stage hand looks around for support but doesn't find any.]

« I'm sorry, » [he pleads.]

" Thieves of my time who repent must still be punished. *Time is a reef,* and all that . . .

[Reluctantly he lays his hands out, palms facing the floor. He knows what's coming. We **all** know what's coming.]

" Left or right? " [the Director demands.]

« Left, make it the left . . . NO, wait! The right!— »

[The Director plunges the samurai vane through the air, cleanly slicing off both the man's hands. They fall to the set-floor like rubber props. Helixes of blood shoot forth from each stump—cue ominous horror movie kill-shot music. The man yowls in agony. Like

Muslim advocates of Islamic law or Sharia, the Director believes that punishment by Hudud is a good way to show that if you go against God, and are a threat to the moral fabric of the community, then you will be severely punished. The Director believes that *he* is God and therefore in the best position to reprimand time-wasters.

« Can I bury my hands? » [the stage hand begs.]

"Amputated limbs don't come under the same ruling as the whole person. They should be put with the garbage."

[A voice from behind the Director shouts something about *Praise be to Allah . . .*]

" Shut up! Now, can SOMEONE *please* GET HIM OFF THE SET! WE DON'T HAVE TIME TO CLEAN UP MORE OF THIS CUNT'S MESS! Nice depth of field, by the way— get an insert. Tell the gaffer I want a Dutch tilt on Klopp, then a deep focus shot. Danny, get the art department on the phone. We need a bounce board to reflect that excess light . . . "

[Klopp and young Stanley watch on.]

• The Director's films are characterised by meta-physical themes and extremely long takes. He used to be an artist, he considers himself an artist still. The more protracted the silence between dialogue the better. Other recurring motifs involve sexuality, murder, guilt, banality, dreams, memory and childhood. By using long takes and few cuts in his films, he aims to give the viewers a sense of time lost and the relationship of one moment in time to another. If his methods are interrupted he punishes people.

[The Director turns back to the crew, winks at Stanley and resumes his position on the stool behind the camera.]

"A-A-A-ND . . . ACTION!"

[Stanley turns to old Klopp with an expression of bewilderment.]

« Who was that? *What's going on?* »

« No one . . . nothing . . . »

■

[The Director starts making right angles with his thumb and forefinger. Stanley is lying in his bunk in Klopp's spare room watching the scene unfold. Klopp is sitting on the toilet with a strained face. The focus-puller is kneeling directly in front of him adjusting his lens. A man holding a large light on a pole creates a dramatic sodium-lit look. The hanging basket outside the bathroom window overflows with pitter-pattering rainwater—4 minute still shot to be edited in later.]

" Let's round this off, people. Let's get this shit done with and move on to the sleep scene. "

[The Director snaps his fingers and a woman brings him a plastic foam cup of coffee. He sips around the rim, and when he brings the cup away from his mouth his moustache is white with froth. Klopp gives one last push and proceeds to wipe.]

" Close up! Then two final takes of the hero sleeping before home-time! " [The Director gets up and starts making more right angles.]

" Good, *good . . .* "

[Stanley wonders what role the Director will have for him in all of this . . .]

■

[The boy wakes up the next morning and the old man

is sitting in the corner of the room, biting his nails.]

« Is everything okay? » [asks the boy.]

« No, no, everything is certainly not okay, Stanley. Everything is far from okay . . . »

« Well, what's wrong? »

« You have to leave. »

« What? Why? »

« Because it's not safe for you here. »

« Why not? »

« Because it's just not! They're not pleased with the introduction of a new character. The Director hates ad-libbing and has said in previous interviews that he hates working with children and animals. He needs everyone to stick to his script, otherwise he, well . . . you *know* what he does. You've seen it for yourself. »

[The boy senses it has something to do with his effect on Klopp's soundtrack.]

« It's the music, isn't it? »

« Amongst other things, yes. You are not welcome here, Stanley, you have to go, at once. He wants to focus his work on exploring the dramatic unities proposed

by his favourite philosopher, Aristotle—the concen-
trated action, happening in one place, within the span
of a single week. »

[The sound of cars pulling up outside indicate that the
crew have arrived to start setting up.]

« Quick, boy! »

[Klopp ushers Stanley out the window. He tells him to
run with emphasised aggression, scaring the boy into
never coming back. The crew come flooding in without so much as a *Hello* or *By your way*. Equipment
spills off the back of Lorries and out of zip bags—
wires, poles, and the various twinkling bulbs of
technology lay strewn across the limited floor space
of Klopp's cottage. Workers are chatting loudly,
laughing and farting.

The Director is talking to his producer.]

" In this manuscript, the one you're reading right now,
I've heard there are a number of stories that inter-
weave with the main text. That sounds like a cop-out.
I'm not sure though, I honestly haven't read the full
manuscript. I know we go to Cannes and I'm sure
Klopp proves a great success, but beyond that . . . not a
scintilla. "

[The Director sits on a hovering dolly and dictates to

the crew.]

" I don't like the cushions, they're too vibrant. Colour
should be used mainly to emphasize certain
moments, but not all the time as this distracts the
viewer. "

[A young girl appears and snatches the cushions from
the sofa.]

" I'm not sure about this wall-art, it's too . . . protestant.
Klopp is Catholic, through and through. "

« Is that in the script? » [asks the producer.]

" No, it's not in the fucking script. But this is *my* production, you flea brain. I decided here, just now, that
he is Catholic, through and through. The Writer and I
have an understanding. Now replace this at once with
an image of Guido Reni's archangel Michael trampling
Satan. "

« We can get *The Crucifixion of Saint Peter*, gaffer . . . »

" That'll do . . . "

« Shall we lighten this chandelier, gaffer? » [asks the
clapper loader.]

" No, no, the background will be dark so there's no
need. "

« Anything else, gaffer? »

" Can we move this fuckin' mirror? It's causing glare and reflecting the cameraman. "

« The assistant directors usually deal with interior and exterior set design, gaffer. »

" I don't have an assistant director. I am my own assistant director. I am pedantic about the details in my film. I am a fine assistant director. Oh, and stop calling me gaffer, you twat.

« What are we going to do about the music? »

" We need to eliminate the boy, for sure. I'll dub in the music we've lost so far later. Stravinsky, probably. »

[A monograph on old Russian icons lies on the table. The Director picks it up and tears the book in half.]

" This won't work as a prop either. "

« Anything else, sir? »

" I want the experience of this film to be faithful to the script. The Writer is writing as we speak, just as I, the Director, am dictating to his notes. "

« Sir . . . »

" According to my notes, the best way to read this book and this line, and these words that I am currently saying, is to 'lay on a comfortable mattress with your head rested on a pillow stuffed with dove feathers. Put your feet against the wall and wiggle your toes a few times to prevent cramping. Raise the book a few inches from your line of vision. Read near an open window on a summer's day and always make sure the stove is switched off.' That's the benefit of the Writer —the luxury of his craft. He can tell people how to interpret his words and the best possible way to consume them. With my medium, I am reliant on people having read the book with these instructions already. I can't very well have a disclaimer at the start of the picture telling people how to sit on their fuckin' seats in the cinema theatre. "

« Still up for the single ten minute still shot of Klopp sitting in the grass outside naked? »

" Yes, we'll organise that take now. "

« Ten minutes is a long time even for you, sir. »

" I forget who it was that said, 'Juxtaposing a person with an environment that is boundless, collating him with a countless number of people passing by close to him and far away, relating a person to the whole world, that is the meaning of cinema.' "

[A man appears with a cell phone to his ear. He takes it away, covers the mouthpiece with the palm of his hand and addresses the Director.]

« Sir, it's for you. We think it's *The Echo* . . . »

[The Director takes the phone.]

" Yes? "

« John Langsyne at *The Echo* here, tell me about your latest film . . . »

" What I have already filmed is genius. I am pleased with my work so far, and it is all MY work. You see, the past is stable, romantic, a thing to be thought of fondly. The present is like trying to hold a water snake—it slips through your hands. In theory it cannot be isolated, not truly. I can capture the past, but I cannot capture the present. I believe the unique characteristic of cinema as a medium is to take our experience of time and alter it. Unedited movie footage transcribes time in *real time*. I want to freeze the present so I can examine it and experience that same feeling of being in the moment . . . and *you* are ruining all this. "

[The Director hangs up the phone and claps his hands together to begin the day . . .]

■

« Okay, so by placing an X on the gun barrel and using
the video editor graphic overlay track on one frame
we should be able to add in the tracer and muzzle shot
sounds. »

" Do it. I want the scene where the little girl shoots
Klopp's naked, charred corpse to be as jolting as
possible. I *want* it to feel unnecessary and gratuitous."

[A small elderly man approaches the Director with his
white hair parted down the middle in severe
curtains.]

« Sir, from what I can gather the boy has gone. »

" Excellent . . . "

[A woman with spectacles and a t-shirt that says KLOPP
THE MOVIE appears with a clipboard and an envelope
under her arm. She passes the envelope to the
Director.]

« This morning's scenes have arrived. »

" Excellent— " [he tears at the brown envelope and
starts reading. The Director's face becomes an image

of utter disgust. You can hear the extras in the backlot of the studio.]

" The boy . . . we need to bring him back. "

« . . . Sir? »

" He's in the fucking script. Look, right here! Get him back. "

« What about the music? »

" FUCK THE MUSIC! I TOLD YOU, STRAVINSKY, LATER! WE'LL DEAL WITH THAT LATER! "

« Yes sir . . . »

[The Director seizes control of his breathing and stifles the rising panic in his gut. He goes to the cameraman and places a hand on his shoulder.]

" Did you get the script this morning? "

[The cameraman nods.]

" We'll use a very long Steadicam shot of the boy riding his bicycle towards Klopp's house, a long dolly shot side-profile might also give it that sense of urgency. Every single one of my films has at least one long, uncut tracking shot, usually with the camera moving backwards and the actor walking facing the camera.

You know this track-in shot uses a lens of moderate focal length, maybe 85mm or 100mm? "

[The listless cameraman nods.]

" Make it happen. "

« How extreme do we want the wide-angle? »

" So extreme that it'll cause barrel distortion. We'll use both dolly shots and handheld shots. This movie might still be manageable, maybe! "

[The Director motions for Sergei, the Russian cinematographer, to follow him outside. They squeeze through the bustle of crewmen who are lifting paintings and couches, rearranging the interior design to better suit the Director's vision. Outside on the soaking grass is a miniature model set-up of the farm and cottage. There is a figurine of Klopp. The Director kneels down and the cinematographer does the same.]

" So you see, we have Klopp here. He exits the house through the front door. The camera will stay on him from a safe distance before the finale. "

« You mean ze explosion? »

" Yes. The armourer will make sure the weapons are deployed safely. "

« There are a few vays ve can achieve zis. Fiery explosions are usually green screen overlays. Ve can edit in stock footage later. »

" No. I want something authentic. "

« The dangers of shooting real explosions make it prohibitive. Ve could film ze actor in front a green screen? Ze green screen we'd be using has to be flat and uniform in colour. »

" Can you make sure there are no shadows projecting onto the screen? Also make sure that nothing outside the green screen itself shows. "

« When he runs out aflame ve release the little girl from her cage with ze machine gun. I think ve can do sum quite beautiful stuff vith ze scene involving the boy's return too. »

" What do you have in mind, Sergei? "

« Ve can make it coalder lookeeng. »

• Sergei emphasises that he strives for realism, but the Director is so focused on his vision. He wants Sergei to portray psychological truth rather than social realism.

« Ze time oaf day might be a problem. »

" We don't have time to be picky, my friend. "

- Sergei has a heavy reliance on natural light and this complements the Director's geometrically-precise shot composition. The significance of Klopp's actions is often determined by subtle differences in lighting. The Director and his cinematographer have spent weeks gauging the natural light at different times of day. With time and funding running low, all those plans have been scrapped.

« Don't you ever worry about what the Writer thinks of you imposing your personality on his vurk? »

" No. ~~The writer does not hate individualism, he hates anarchism.~~ As long as he can control the majority of what he creates he is happy. He even enjoys the occasional bout of intellectual sparring. He can control me. "

... **(?)**

∎

- The Director describes himself in terms of classical music—he is romantic, passionate, significant, dark, all set up pretty in his second movement of his

seventh symphony, as performed by the Glen
Ommensetter Philharmonic Orchestra. He doesn't
care that people think he's demented because his
mind is so attuned to fantasy, and he is utterly content and compelled by his own inward journey. He
lives in his head and plans on keeping it that way. He
is the auteur.

The Director always has a cold. Even in summer, even
in Hollywood. It's like a plague. His life is depressingly
cinéma vérité.

He is always tugging in his great big trench-coat,
burying his neck beneath the collar. You'll hear him
sniffing hard before you see him coming. For an
entertainer of some esteem he looks pretty embar-
rassing, all greasy hair and pit-stains. But there are
people who think he is ruggedly handsome in an
unwashed, raw kind of way—other actress whores,
mostly.

[The Director clicks the record button on his
Dictaphone.]

" I've seen the dailies, they look okay, answer print is
okay. I could fire everyone on this production if I
wanted to. I can do all the jobs one hundred times
better than they ever could. Take Jerry the sound guy
for example. The studio is paying him £15,000 to do
the sound and editing on this picture. He is respected,

but I can do better. I occupied the sound dept and the lab every night, learned everything I could about sound, film developing and copying. It's only because it's fundamentally impossible for one single man to do all the work on a movie that I can't, but I could, if I wanted to. If I REALLY wanted to . . . But I do need Sergei. Sergei is a genius, my kindred spirit. The cinematographer selects the film stock, lens, filters. It's Sergei's job to realize the scene in accordance with the intentions of *my* vision. He also acts as my creative consultant. If he were incapable I wouldn't use him. I allow him complete control; I won't specify exact camera placement and lens selection. I forget who it was that said, 'Life stretches in a cruel but voluptuous arc from birth to death, a meaningless journey', but it's relevant and it's why I make films. It's all about the exposition, the character back story that makes *Klopp* tangible. "

■

[Stanley appears in the distance. His legs are a blur as tears vein each side of his face—the sheer velocity of Stanley's cycling creates a maelstrom of dust in his wake. He believes he is returning to Klopp's house because he is worried about the old man's well-being,

as if of his own freewill. The truth of the matter is that
it is the Writer who has reintroduced Stanley's character into proceedings, and that no part of the boy's
decision to return has been his own. The Director
spots the boy and signals to the cameraman to focus
in on his arrival. The sun is a sphere—blister-bright, a
Roman cloak over the entire set.]

" This reminds me of a scene from my first picture,
where the heroine races to the abortion clinic after
her father, played by me, impregnates her . . . "

[Stanley screeches to a halt right in front of the crew.
He sees the camera on him.]

« Klopp? *Klopp?* » [the boy yells, ignoring the group of
filmmakers as best he can.]

[Klopp is sitting at the table with his head in his hands,
pale as an autumnal moon. The sad panpipe music
swirls around his skull like a noisy, agitated fly. His
neck aches and he hasn't been allowed to bathe in
months. Klopp finds his own stink nauseating. He
hears the boy's voice and shoots up from his stool,
which goes careening across the room. The boy bursts
in the door and sees the old man standing. The music
stops. Stanley looks at Klopp the way a pet owner
looks at a demented, dying animal.]

« Stanley, you have to get out of here. Haven't you read the script? »

« No . . . I . . . no, I can't. »

[The Director appears with a handheld camera clutched up to his right eye.]

« Stanley, I'm to be burned alive . . . »

« Then why are you still here? I don't get it? Make me understand? None of this makes any sense to me? Maybe it's cos I'm a boy and I don't understand the world yet, I don't know. Come with me to my father's estate. He won't mind, or at least I think I can persuade him to give you as a job as a gardener. »

« I'm not skilled enough. »

« Then just leave! »

« I can't, you see it's that simple, I just can't! »

« I don't understand. You know you're to be burned alive and yet you *want* to stay? »

« It's not about what I want . . . »

« Of course it is! »

« No, Stanley, look—have you actually read the script? »

« I told you, no. »

« Then how can I do anything about it? Answer me that one question? Answer it? Go? »

« Just leave! Go out the front door, walk a half a mile down the road to the market, do *something*! »

« They planned for you to come here . . . »

« You mean this has been a trap? »

« Not as such, no, not as such. You are a character. You're at the mercy of the written word. »

" OKAY, LET'S GET THE LAST SCENE DONE! MAKE SURE THE BOY SEES EVERYTHING, " [the Director intervenes.] " Okay people, let's get the 'Abby Singer' before our big denouement. "

[Two men appear and lift Stanley up by his armpits to remove him from the cottage. Klopp follows.

[Stanley screams back at Klopp,] « GET OUT OF HERE! GET OUT OF HERE YOU SENILE OLD COOT! » [but Klopp just stands in the doorway like a dead-eyed mannequin amid a wreath of smoke. He begins to undress, just like in the script. The boy cannot budge his arms from the vice-tight grip of the men. Stanley hears the sad music for the first time. He senses the desperate sorrow in the soundtrack. The boy knows

something terrible is about to happen. Klopp raises
one hand to wave goodbye before a voice in the
distance yells] " NOW! DO IT NOW! " [and the house
begins billowing smoke from the roof. A flurry of
crewmen rush out from each side of the cottage but
Klopp stays in the doorway as if he couldn't move
even if he wanted to. The boy watches on, tears half
filling his eyes as the flames start to form and consume the entire left side of the cottage. The blaze is
vicious, it devours everything as it spreads in jagged
triangles of orange and black. Smoke rises as high as
the twisted clouds overhead until the sky is just a
burnt river of impending destiny. Stanley sees the
flames reach the wood on the porch then catch the
bottom of Klopp's trouser leg. His face is still unemo-
tional, almost absent-minded. The fiery streak races
up the trouser leg and scorches his arm into a well-
cooked log of bone—then the fire reaches his face.
The boy sees the veil of Klopp's flesh whittle away like
a damaged film reel. Shreds of skin peel off in great
charred strips. Stanley half expects to see a robotic
skeleton or blank dressmaker's doll-face beneath. The
boy realises that Klopp is, in fact, an immitant; an
artificial humanoid created by the studio. This
knowledge does nothing to diminish his feeling of
grief. After a few minutes slowly barbequing, Klopp
walks out into the lawn as a burnt polymorph, drops
to his knees and falls to his side—dead.]

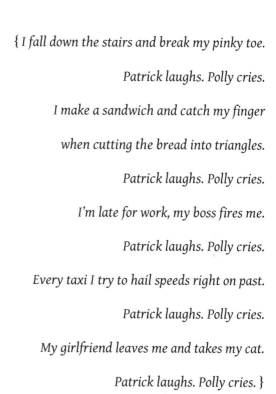

{ *I fall down the stairs and break my pinky toe.*

Patrick laughs. Polly cries.

I make a sandwich and catch my finger

when cutting the bread into triangles.

Patrick laughs. Polly cries.

I'm late for work, my boss fires me.

Patrick laughs. Polly cries.

Every taxi I try to hail speeds right on past.

Patrick laughs. Polly cries.

My girlfriend leaves me and takes my cat.

Patrick laughs. Polly cries. }

[The Director gives a cue to a little girl holding a
machine gun. She walks nervously into view of the
camera with the giant weapon resting on her
shoulder, does her best to lift the gun to an angle
directly above Klopp's cooked body. She fires three
times, the third shot knocking her back into a puddle
of mud. She starts to cry. A woman runs on set, scoops
up the little girl and carries her off-camera. Stanley
does his best to understand, but there is no justice or

sense in the imaginary playground created by these
people.]

[Close up of the boy's tortured face.]

[A cameraman zooms in on Stanley. He stares into the
lens intensely. Were he not an eight-year-old boy, the
Director could've been jolted into an inner-anxiety.
There is revenge in his stare.]

" WE GOT IT! CUT, PEOPLE! "

[The men restraining Stanley drop him and he lands in
a wet pathway of dirt. The crew set up to leave, and
the Director and his Russian cinematographer seem
to have vanished. We are left with a scene of a distant
city through a wreath of fog, Isometric projections
appearing behind a cardboard countryside landscape,
a faded rainbow arching over it all . . .]

[The smell of plastic and metal and smoke is
unbearable.]

TWO

[Shapes of light arrive through the heady wine of sleep.

The Director gets up, spatters his bathroom with blood-polluted liquid faeces, washes himself with carbolic soap and electrocutes himself with a jigger of black coffee ...

It is the night before Super-Cannes. He smells of shredded tobacco and gush of sperm—a man who walks and talks with an eternal throbbing prick against his belly, a yearning to be both immortally present and spectral at once. By all accounts, a walking, talking, spunking, immortally-spectral little prick. A genius.

Mist lifts from beyond the field and the dens of the Zinc Theatre emerge from its mantle.]

" Fuckin' shit hole. "

[He goes to the back door of his condo and stands,
   shirtless, looking out at the ugly town that rests
   behind the alien-made stockades. He coughs,
   scratches his pubis and grooms a cigarette. The
   Director gets through most days in a brainless
   trance—when he isn't directing, at least.]

• The Director walks with a limp these days because
   there is a mercury bullet lodged in his shin. It came
   from a woman's gun, a woman from the past. They
   often used to pump each other full of lead and since
   she shot him back, he feels like he might actually love
   her. He can't remember her name but it starts with an
   'M' and ends with an 'OTHER'.

[He goes out to the coup, scatters grain for the
   chickens. The grain is made mostly of broken up
   oyster shell, potato skins, eggplant leaves and bug-
   softened zucchini, but there are shaving of human
   flesh in there too. Chickens have a strange pre-
   eminence to them; the Director thinks it could be
   because of their distant relation to the Winged-
   Shaver-Gangle.

Vessels run through him like rivers of bad plasma. He
glares at one chicken with livery yellow eyes. It has a
letter stuck to the back of its neck. He tries to catch up

with it to retrieve the note, but it ducks away every
time.]

" Sly little fuck, aren't ya? "

[It walks with an exaggerated strut, just like the
Director. He eventually catches it by the leg and rings
its neck with two twists. He pulls the letter from the
limp chicken.]

Dear fellow functional alcoholic,

*My name is Ignius Ellis. I'm not a nice man, in fact, I'm a
bloody horrible cunt, but there is a great injustice that I
cannot go on ignoring any longer. I know we live on the
opposite ends of the earth, but the State will come for you
too.*

*The Slave State seeks to control the means of production
and extract surplus labour value of human beings—
apparently invisible 4rth dimension labour is the cheapest
way to satisfy themselves spiritually and emotionally—me,
I'd much prefer grabbing a pint and watching the football
on telly, but I'm a bit of a pacifist that way.*

I propose we wage unrestricted drone warfare

DOWN WITH THE STATE!! (too much?)

[The Director scrunches up the paper ball and tosses it.]

" Parasitic Slave State trash . . . "

[The sun beats down onto the black loam of Hollywood,
  its yellow shroud glittering the puddles and half-
  lighting the faces of slave-people in the park. Coca-
  Cola trucks emerge from their loading docks and two
  good-looking college girls share inconsequential chit-
  chat—the Director thinks out loud to himself that,
  'Christ, we really have no sense of irony', then remembers
  he's living in a young country and forgives the naïve
  innocence that once grated on him so heavily.]

■

• Words are funny things, aren't they? Words. Even the
  word "word" is funny . . . "funny." What does "funny"
  even mean?

[On the train to Super-Cannes, the Director and his
  producer are sitting in a booth while patting each
  other on the back for a job well done. The train is
  shaking furiously along the rusted sleepers. They
  fully expect to rake in the awards. The producer is an
  unreasonably fussy man who the Director reluctantly
  puts up with. He has the face of an ugly man: caved-in,

bug eyes bulging behind swollen cornrowed lids. The producer's lips are like puckering trout and the boulder of skull rests on top of a hard, fat physique. The Director has always been fascinated by his ugliness. He is wasted as a storm-fucked meadow. The Director often fantasises about murdering him with his samurai sword, but his contract wouldn't allow it. Even if he could prove the producer was just a stinking immitant, it still wouldn't wash.]

« Why did we have to get the Eurostar from St. Pancras? We could've gotten to Super-Cannes by actually staying in France, » [the producer whines while tweaking the tip of a hypodermic needle. He rolls up his shirt sleeve and bites his lip in preparation for the shot of precious junk syrup.]

" Because it would take five hours by high-speed TGV train from Paris. "

[A woman pushes a dining cart along the hallway. She stops at the Director's vestibule and offers him a selection of alcohol. She is too attractive to be real. She's so thin you can hear every cough rattle in her chest. Upon closer inspection, each limb looks slightly out of joint.

Immitants often suffer from an abnormal skin complaint where little black islets stand out, ugly and raised from the surface. The woman's red lips bud out in stark contrast to the beige artifice of her flesh.

The producer stuffs the large bleeding needle down the side of his chair and unfurls his shirt sleeve while swearing under his breath—he *hates* being interrupted. The Director takes a glass of merlot but the producer is still unhappy with the route they've taken to get to the festival. The anticipation of waiting to get a hit worsens his mood. The woman leaves.]

« What's the point, I mean, I just don't get why we got the Eurostar? »

" We'll get there quicker, you see, it all makes perfect sense if you just engage your brain. "

« But the festival isn't until tomorrow night! »

" It gives us a chance to soak up the atmosphere, gives you a chance to *recharge your batteries.* " [The Director is half convinced the producer is an immitant.]

« Pah! Atmosphere? It'll just be the usual clutch of film industry folks bitching about each other before the awards. When we take this movie to the hard-tops, that's when we'll see the real big bucks. »

[The Director breathes slowly, tries to stay calm. He is almost at the zenith of his patience.]

" Why don't we take a stroll down the Promenade de la Croisette? "

« Whatever you want. »

" I got a letter from Thomas Gale. It's the first chapter of his memoir. "

« Ah Thomas, how is the old toad? »

" You've never met Thomas . . . "

« What do you m—–? I mean, of *course* I have . . . »

" No, you haven't, you were supposed to meet him, three times in fact. You didn't turn up once. "

« Well, I KNOW who Thomas Gale is, don't I? »

" I suppose you do . . . "

« Exactly. »

" Shall I read it to you? "

« Yes, yes. Do, do . . . »

" Ahem . . . "

> **Polly Laughs, Patrick Cries**
>
> *I fall down the stairs and break my pinky toe. Polly laughs. Patrick cries.*
>
> *I make a sandwich and catch my finger when cutting the bread into triangles. Polly laughs. Patrick cries.*
>
> *I'm late for work, my boss fires me. Polly laughs. Patrick cries.*
>
> *Every taxi I try to hail speeds right*

[The Director averts his gaze from the letter and the swirling red sediments of his drink. He sees the producer spiking the veiny curve of his forearm. His sulk picks up instantly, as if the drug he'd been feeding himself intravenously were possessed of surplus mood stabilisers. *He might just be real after all.*]

[The idea of sightseeing in Super-Cannes is now something to be looked forward to.]

« Super-Cannes, eh? With its lovely border of palm trees and beaches of alabaster sand? »

" Exactly, exactly! That's the spirit. Do some window shopping in the high-end boutiques or admire the luxury hotels. "

« Are we in the Carlton or the Hôtel Martinez? »

" Neither, it'll be the Majestic or the Hilton. "

[The producer's brief positivity evaporates.]

« Pah, bloody Hilton! I *bet* we get lumped with the Hilton! »

" You could have a drink at the terrace. They let you do that there. "

« I don't want to drink on the terrace! Does my room have a balcony? »

" You better pray it doesn't, you fucking philistine . . . "

[The producer doesn't hear this, he's too busy speaking in a strange tongue that turns out to be Esperanto. The Director doesn't like the producer saying things in a language he can't understand.]

" Did you hear? They want to induct me into all sorts of nonsense now, all sorts, yes. Since the last picture, I'm already a member of the Académie française and The Royal Academy of Belgium. "

[The producer turns sour again. Like a Salvador Dali clock, his face melts into formlessness and maintains only a semblance of human expression.]

« What for? Why aren't I being inducted? »

" Because you haven't actually *done* anything, Mr Producer. "

« I helped you get financed. »

" You didn't even watch the final cut. "

« I didn't have to! That's not my job! »

" What exactly *is* your job? "

« Well, I . . . there are a lot of things you don't see going on . . . behind the scenes. The entire production would fall to pieces without me, okay, Ommensetter? »

" I'm sure your contribution was absolutely crucial. Do not call me that. "

« Why not? That's your name. »

" It was never my name, you ingrate. Or should I call you Ivan? "

[The producer tries to move past this topic before the subject of identity comes up.]

« So . . . why aren't I being given lots of things? »

[The Director pulls out an envelope with a royal seal, broken.]

" I got this just this morning, " [the Director plays with the envelope, weaving the long edge between his fingers. He opens it and unfolds a creased letter.]

" As of next month, I'll be a Member of the Mallarmé Academy, Austria-German Academy, American Academy, Mark Twain Academy, Honorary President of the Super-Cannes Film Festival, Honorary President of the France-Hungary Association and President of the Jazz Academy. "

[He looks at the producer with a cruel smugness. He knows this will worsen his feeling of inferiority, and that is completely the Director's intention. He has to know his place in all this.]

" I forget who it was that said, 'Art washes away from the soil, the dust of everyday life'. "

« If all goes to plan the winners card will read as follows: »

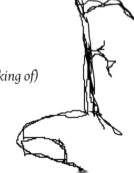

Palme d'Or – Klopp

Grand Prix – Klopp

Prix du Jury – Klopp

Palme d'Or du court métrage – Klopp (making of)

Prix d'interprétation masculine – Klopp

Prix de la mise en scène – The Director
Prix du scénario – The Writer
Prix Un Certain Regard – Stanley
Caméra d'Or – Klopp
Prix de la FIPRESCI – Klopp

« Apparently the President of the Jury this year is Dr Chopin, » [the producer says this while reading Thomas Gale's letter.]

" Chopin is a boor of a man. "

« Least it's not Dr Van Klee. That fuckin' crazed scalpel-jockey is sick in the head. I hear he fucks robots? Can you believe that? *Robots!* »

" Immitants, actually, and haven't we all? "

« What? Fucked robots? »

[The producer thinks about this for a second before admitting that, indeed, he *had* fucked his share of artificial pussy.]

« Okay, I'll give you that, but Van Klee, there's something unwholesome about him. »

" Rich coming from a producer who sold his kids into slavery. "

« Hey, don't even … »

" Don't even what? Mention that? Don't be so judge-mental then, it doesn't suit you. "

« Those kids were no good in civilised society. They belong in slavery, it'll build their character. »

" You're not wrong there, no sir. "

[The Director's cell phone rings. There is a weeping woman on the other line.]

« Glen, is that you? » [she asks, her throat hoarse.]

" Yes, who is this? "

« It's Isabella. »

" Isabella? "

« You don't remember me? »

" Jesus honey, I meet at least a half dozen Isabella's every day! "

« The famous one. »

" The famous one? AAAHHH, *Isabella*, how are you? "

« I'm . . . fine, where are you? »

" On my way to Super-Cannes. "

« With your latest film? God, I'm so sorry, I can call you again . . . »

" No, please Isabella, I could use the change of
   conversation . . . "

« I feel just awful. »

" About what? "

« Not telling you. »

" Not telling me what? Wait . . . What, you're *not* . . . ?
   Are you? "

« No, no! »

" Thank Christ for that. I'm not paying for *another*
   abortion. "

« No, it's just . . . that night we spent together, do you
   recall? »

" Hmm . . . vaguely. I remember cheap wine and an
   after-party for some television pilot. "

« It was your sister's wedding. We fooled around in the,
   um . . . »

" Yes, yes. I remember. "

« You raped me in the end. »

" As I've said, I remember. "

« Well, it's just, and bearing in mind I do feel just awful about telling you this, especially on your way to a big film festival, but . . . »

" Come on woman, spit it out already! "

« I have chlamydia. »

" So? "

« So, I think you might have it too. »

" Is that it? "

« Yes, and like I said, I feel really terrible about it. I know how important you are and I hope it won't stop you casting me again in the future . . . »

" I found a genital wart about a week ago, I'm hardly bothered. "

« Then you're really not mad? »

" Isabella, darling, chances are I passed that virus onto *you*. "

« Goodness, that is a relief. I can't tell you how scared I was . . . »

" Well, if that's all . . . "

« Wait! There is one other thing. »

" Yes? " [Sighs.]

« Do you want to be with me? »

" Do I *what??* "

« Want to be with me? »

" Fuck no! "

« It's just, well . . . that night was . . . »

" I have to go. "

« Please, just tell me. I'll leave you alone if it's a
rejection. »

" You could deal with a complete rejection right now? "

« Well, no, but I want to know. I'll just have to deal with
it. »

" Why are you doing this? "

« Because I want to know. I have to start rebuilding my
life without you. »

" Don't do this now. I'll call you later. "

« Then it's a *no* . . . »

" I didn't even say that. I mean, I did, but . . . "

« You should just say it. Tell me to go. »

" Stop it, Isabella. "

« No. You have no idea how much I love you. »

" Christ, Isabella . . . "

« I knew you'd scoff at me, undermine my emotions. »

" You are *not* in love with me. "

« I am in love with you. »

" You don't love anyone, Isabella. Nobody loves anyone anymore, so just stop this . . . "

« Well, I love you! I can't stop thinking about you; about waking up next to you and your trophy cabinet, your bulging trophy cabinet . . . I'd live in your trophy cabinet, you know? I'd be so quiet you'd barely hear my breath against the glass. I swear. Just let me live with you in your trophy cabinet. »

" There's no way I'm *that* good a fuck! "

« It's not about that, this is about love. »

" It's *always* about *that* . . . "

« No. »

" Okay, I've tried being civil with you . . . "

« No . . . »

" No what? "

« Don't yell at me. »

" Fucking hell, Isabella, you're a fucking mess. "

« I know, but I do love you. »

" You called me to tell me you love me and that I have chlamydia? "

« I *called* you because I don't know what else to do. »

" I think you know what you ought to do. "

« You mean you'd let me do it? In good conscience, you'd let me kill myself? »

" Conscience? What is this, woman? You're ruining my night, I should be jubilant but that's not exactly easy when you have a hysterical, washed-up whore on the phone prattling on about love and chlamydia! "

« I didn't mean to ruin your night. »

" Then kill yourself. "

« I shouldn't have called. »

" No, you shouldn't have. "

« Please believe me that I love you. »

" You're starting to rile me, Isabella. I'm hanging up. "

« No, wait! »

" I'm hanging up now . . . "

■

« Who wrote the libretto for *Klopp*? » [the producer
asks while looking over the nominee cards.]

" I don't know, " [the Director admits.]

« Well, it's up for best original score. I don't think
anyone realised it was from an Igor Stravinsky's
opera-oratorio, which had its original May time performance in the Theatre Sarah Bernhardt in Paris. »

" Was it Cocteau? "

« It wasn't the Beastie Boys? »

" Don't know. Doubt it, those guys don't do high art, do
they? Maybe, I don't know. Put my name down anyway. They'll never research it. "

« Pancake Patterson's jazz score was genius, a real
contender. »

" Pancake Patterson is a nobody, " [hisses the Director,
who only met Patterson once and decided he was a

pretentious shit. Of course, he deduced this solely
from his style and syncopated walk. Patterson had a
pencil moustache and dressed garishly, he was the
kind of jerk you'd see dancing wildly to jazz or bebop
in old 50's America. His shirt and thick soled suede
shoes the only things more starched than his
unswerving loyalty to liberal ideals.]

« I guess he is a nobody. »

" Raymond Hogg wants to work with me apparently. "

« Who's that again? »

" Raymond Hogg, he's a real writer who penned
'Bucolic Musings in the Snake Lair' but who was
argued out of existence by a radical network of
revolutionaries, mail artists, poets, performers,
underground 'zines, cybernauts and squatters. Hogg's
name became a nom de plume for the movement who
denied he ever really existed in order to take credit
for his work. "

« Ha . . . »

[Sergei, who had been in the opposite booth, appears at
the window. The Director waves him in. Sergei has a
brown envelope under his arm.]

" What's that? " [asks the Director, gesturing to the
envelope with his glass.]

« It's the latest script from the Writer. »

" Give me that! " [The Director snatches the rectangular package from the Russian cinematographer.]

« I can't believe he's finished the next part already! I mean, wow! » [the producer adds, a little more soberly. The Director's face is warped with confusion as he takes in the first scene of the latest script.]

" Wah? It's like the words on the page are dancing. I feel like a dyslexic trying to make sense of small print hieroglyphics on a faulty roller coaster ride! "

« Try and focus . . . » [Sergei insists.]

" I'm trying. I just can't make head nor tail of it. "

« Persevere, it's totally worth it. »

" Okay . . . "

[The Director screws up his eyes and holds the script at varying distances from his face. He eventually gives up and slams the manuscript shut.]

" Let me look over this properly tomorrow. There's too much to celebrate now. Tonight, we drink! "

[The Director raises his samurai sword into the air theatrically, like a musketeer.]

« We've still to organise the Director's commentary for the special edition DVD . . . »

" Please, no cinema parlance, we have guests! " [The Director gestures to the blonde haired trolley-girl who has stopped outside the booth. She sees the Director placing his samurai in the overhead luggage compartment and bites her bottom lip. The producer is babbling something about a corporate conspiracy involving the bones of World War II American GIs being used as charcoal cigarette filters.]

■

(*At the Super-Cannes after-party*)

" The late great jazz musician Peter 'Pancake' Patterson. "

[The Director extends his hand and meets with the legend's assured grip. The flesh feels man-made. Pancake Patterson's face is a sketchbook of whorls, his cheeks scored with the scars of rancorous life lessons—*or bad craftsmanship?*]

" I'm a big fan, BIG fan, " [lies the Director.]

« Sorry your picture didn't win anything. Bunch of mugs this lot anyway. »

[The Director looks at Patterson with a hateful glare.]

" And congratulations on winning best soundtrack, Pancake. Maybe we can collaborate sometime. "

« Thanks, me ol' son. »

[The producer appears, stoned and disorientated.]

« Where are we? »

" At the Super-Cannes after party. "

« Good night? »

" Not really, no. We won a total of, um . . . what was it again? . . . ah yes, NO awards and I forgot my genital wart cream. I'm itching like a flea ridden polecat! "

« We won *nothing*? »

" No. Where were you anyway? "

« I had this dream where I was walking through the thrown ramparts of a destroyed city of soggy, wilting cardboard . . . the ruins beneath my feet . . . the awful, consuming shadow and sense of dread . . . »

" Be quiet. "

« A woman was looking for you. »

" What woman? "

« Was that Pancake Patterson I saw you talking to? »

" What woman?? "

« Isabella or something. She has weed. »

[The Director turns sharply to face his producer. He
seizes his collar and pulls him in.]

" Isabella is *here?* "

« I just said that . . . »

" Are you sure it's her? I mean, she said her name was
Isabella? "

[The producer gives a lazy nod to confirm.]

" Jesus, I have to get out of here. *Time is a fucking prison,
and all that* . . . "

[Isabella is waiting outside. A gust of wind sends a
hoard of swirling debris a hundred feet into the air.
She's wearing a hooded anorak and slink lambskin
gloves that she bought for a bargain price down the
high street. Gropecunt Lane is a decaying region of
Super-Cannes, littering it's avenues with the red
paper lanterns of prosperous sex tourism.

As the Director pushes through the clump of
Hollywood stars and movie execs, a large, hairy hand
grabs him by the shoulder, halting him suddenly. He
turns around slowly. The hard, cracked pavement of
Albert Mordecai's face is staring back.]

« Can we have a chat? »

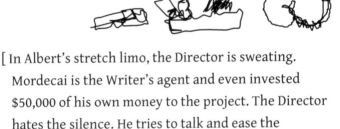

[In Albert's stretch limo, the Director is sweating.
Mordecai is the Writer's agent and even invested
$50,000 of his own money to the project. The Director
hates the silence. He tries to talk and ease the
atmosphere.]

" The boy is the main character . . . I think it's genius. "

« *What?* » [Mordecai snarls back.]

" The Writer's latest screenplay. I re-read it, it's
genius. "

« Come now, 'genius' is to say life-altering. It's *good*,
day-changing at best. »

" What about the ending when Stanley jumps from the building and somersaults five times before landing safely in a deli-stand . . . ? "

« Okay, granted, that *was* genius given the events that'd gone before . . . what with him losing his legs and all. »

" We need to find the boy again, get him in for a meeting. The little fuck won't believe his luck! "

« Listen, the Writer isn't happy, and when the Writer isn't happy, I'm not fuckin' happy, ya dig? »

" I dig . . . "

[Mordecai's car phone rings.]

« Excuse me while I take this. »

[Mordecai answers and rests his head on the padded cushion behind him. The Director can see right up the snotty canals of his large hook nose.]

« Sheila, is that you? »

[Squeaky voice confirms.]

« Okay, uh-huh . . . uh-huh . . . okay . . . but no women in this one. »

« *Why?* »

« I hate all women. »

« *You mean you hate feminists?* »

« No, I *mean* I hate *all* women. Male sympathisers are
just as bad as feminists. Sympathisers colonise the
male identity and rape our bodies by reducing real
masculinity to an artefact, appropriating all gender
for themselves. If feminism were to ever move beyond naturalism and essentialism then I'd listen to it,
but the obsession with identity politic means it can
never, and *will* never, move away from the oedipal
narrative. »

[Squeaky voice agrees and apologises for some
reason.]

[Mordecai slams the phone back onto the receiver.]

« Where were we? »

" I'm learning Esperanto. " [The Director brings out an
old dirty handkerchief and dabs at the sides of his
mouth and under his leaking nostrils. He twists and
arches his back until he hears the 'snick' of his
vertebrae re-positioning.]

« No, that wasn't it . . . »

" I've decided I'll do the picture. The script is tough, but as you rightly pointed out, it is brilliant. I think we can track down the Stanley kid if . . . "

« Yeah, that was what we were talking about. About that . . . »

" What? "

« He doesn't want you to direct . . . »

" *What??* "

« The Writer, he wants Sergei to direct with LaMotte producing. »

" But . . . it was a frame-for-frame enactment! "

« He thinks you changed too much of his script. He said it was too arty. You tried to introduce meaning where there was none. He just wanted senseless shit to happen, simple enough. You know his saying, '*This is not the generation for the vulnerable or sensitive individual, you can't survive that way, not anymore . . .*' »

[Mordecai is sitting in his chair with an angry expression weighing heavy on his tight, moustachioed upper lip. Bleach pale eyes skirt the bridge of his boathook nose; Mordecai unzips his training jacket until spiny troll hair pops out.]

" Give me a second chance, this is my first time working with the Writer, I'll get it right next time, " [begs the Director.]

« Second chances? *Second chances?* Let me tell you about second chances! »

" Albert, come on . . . "

« This one time, before being absorbed into the 4rth dimension, I was out jogging through Central Park from East 86th Street to East 96th, that's when I first saw this guy—a big burly creature, shoulders hunched, quads bulging out from behind sweat-saturated gym shorts. I spotted him well off in the distance. The brutish size of him was enough to snare my attention. He was jogging towards me, parallel, past the Central Park reservoir, away from the erec-tiles of Manhattan. As he got closer I realised the narrow path would eventually push us side by side and in that unintended concord, I would have to come to the fore. He hulked around the corner of the mesh fence and I smiled wanly and mumbled, 'Morning . . . ' He smiled back with considerable confidence and boomed, 'MORNIN'!'

« I don't mind telling you that this tiny acknowl-edgment made my morning, made my day even. This

extraordinary specimen noticed *me*, ME—Albert
Mordecai!

« Well fuck, what can I say, my mind ran amok—I was
his pal now, we'd hang out, grab a beer, do laundry,
blow smoke rings together, shoot hoops—we were
gym buddies within the week in my crazy fuckin'
imagination. I saw him help me regain my dwindling
self-esteem; he'd protect me from bigger more
threatening men because, of course, I reminded him
of what he used to be like before he scaled the seemingly impossible heights of physical fitness. I prayed
we'd cross paths again.

« At 9 a.m. I was out jogging past the shabby tene-
ments and townhouses of East Harlem fantasising
about my kindred brother when, there, I saw him in
the distance. 'Morning', I mumbled, but with greater
range and self-assurance than our first meeting. The
jogger smiled and replied 'MORNIN'' almost twice as
confident and booming as before. I almost stopped
jogging, but saw that he had no intention of looking
back or interrupting his fitness schedule. Fair
enough, I thought, but another encouraging en-
counter. At home that night, I made love to my wife
like I've never made love to her before. I was buoyant,
it was obvious why.

« The following day I was patrolling *our* route and had a
feeling things were suddenly different. There was a
swelling in the pit of my stomach that sensed
something unwelcome afoot (my bowls possess a
clairvoyant intuition, rarely ever proven wrong). It
got to 9:10 a.m. and I had been hopping on the same
spot by a lamppost outside the Metro North Plaza,
there's still no sign of my guy. Words cannot describe
the bitter disillusionment I was left with as a result of
this no-show. I called in sick to work then went home
and beat my wife within an inch of her life with a
studded belt. She couldn't believe the radical change
in me, but I was absolutely fuckin' livid. The next day,
I was driving to work when I saw him jogging past our
usual meeting place. I honked the horn and flipped
him off. I wasn't sure if he saw me. 'HEY, ASSHOLE?' I
yelled—but nothing. He had these massive head-
phones on so I got out of the car and sprinted towards
him. In my angry haste I completely forgot that I'd
abandoned my vehicle in the middle of crosstown
traffic. Still I pumped after him, deftly avoiding
pedestrians and screeching taxi cabs. I was gaining on
him, the continent of sweat that sluiced his upper
back was within touching distance. I put my hand out,
straightened at the elbow, and as my fingertips
touched the soft fabric of the hood of his sweater,
something clattered into me. A taxi cab . . . »

" Wow . . . "

« Shut up and fuckin' listen. I opened my eyes and as the blurry mist of semi-consciousness became clearer, I saw him. He was staring directly into my eyes, into my soul. An overwhelming wave of peace and joy lapped over me.

« 'Morning', he said as he noticed me coming to. You know what I said to him? »

" No? "

« I said, 'Suck my dick, asshole . . .' »

" Okay . . . "

« What I'm saying is, you only get one chance, you little worm, before I flip you off and chase you down the fuckin' street, ya dig? »

{ *There is an evil sect of Hollywood trying to kill you all, man. It's the same fuckin' sinister organization that killed Heath Ledger, David Carradine, and Chris Penn. Let me tell ya, it's also responsible for extorting millions from their bank accounts and running them out of the fuckin' country. It's true. Ommensetter will be next. They'll make a fake probate file, create an identity from a recently deceased woman, also with the surname Ommensetter, and use a fake trust fund to* deposit and cash the Ommensetter royalty checks. Only, the old Ommensetter woman is real—she is worth $60 million.

I know all this is going to happen because I am the Writer. I eventually left the stage. I had to, I am not an actor. I had no idea how I got there, to be honest. I'd begged at His feet once before; I wasn't going to do it again.

The chorus of boos and jackal laughter filled me up to the brim. I couldn't lift my head from the hangdog position. Life was made of moments like this when I was an actor. My shoes were blurry behind a mesh of adult tears. I yearned. I was a yearning machine. No one could've known this, of course. No one could have possibly understood the loneliness that stretched and thinned me every waking hour of every day. So I left the stage saturated in the apathy I'd come to expect. I left him there, on the stage. I promised myself I'd never be laughed at, I'd be the wizard behind the curtain, not the puppet on the stage being pelted by rotten fruit.

I watched the man I used to be.

They flipped me over and tugged my hair until the roots squealed against the scalp. The immitant audience parted my buttocks, smeared its metallic cock with axle grease and probed around the anal cavity until the tip met the warmth of my lower intestine.

Do it to me, I mouthed into their palm.

A pearlescent geyser followed. The man I used to be . . .

He tossed the golden guitar across his dressing room as a reflected image of himself fractured into a million potsherds of clean glass. He felt his space suddenly compromised. He thought of the boy who looked like him, the girl who'd dropped him so effortlessly, the trusts obliterated. The audience were still there and they knew it all, found their way backstage like a liquid-metal predator. Still he yearned an unquenchable yearning, I saw him yearning—the machine that could not be controlled. My pen ran out of ink, the author still didn't stop writing. As a young writer I was part of the famous AD-JECTIVES—a group who informally adopted and shared Raymond Hogg's work. It was used by hundreds of artists and activists all over the Slave State and the Americas since the first failed emancipation. The pseudo-name first appeared in the town of Moosejaw when a number of cultural activists began using it while staging a series of urban and media pranks and to experiment with new forms of authorship and identity. Our multiple-use name spread to other Slave towns and cities, Wire and Shell County, as well as countries outside the Slave-zone such as Austria-Germany, New Catalonia, and Soviet-Asia. We waged a guerrilla warfare on the cultural industry, ran unorthodox solidarity campaigns for victims of the Slave State's censorship policies, repression and, above all, played out elaborate media pranks as a form of art. Now I'm content writing bullshit for

Joe Blow . . . }

• The same sun that brings out the lilies brings out the snakes.

« So . . . what the fuck was that all about? »

[Davie Sock sits his copy of this manuscript, open, over his lap. His pal Ali finishes the last page and grunts. His face is one of confounded disgust.]

« I . . . don't know. What a pile of shit, man! » [Ali tosses the book into one of those trash receptacles they have around campus. A bird disgorges a lightening white trail of shit over the book almost on cue. A student called Gottlieb, who was about to reach for the book, recoils his hand just in time. Davie studies the blurb on the back cover and flips through the novella as if trying to locate the exact point where his bafflement turned to sheer frustration—then finally, unmitigated fury. He can't articulate his feelings.]

« But . . . I . . . we . . . » [Davie holds the book out in front of him, between thumb and forefinger, like a stinking dead mackerel.]

« Don't, Davie, honestly. Let's just try and move on with our lives.

« How much did this cost again? »

« Fuck knows, Grievesy suggested it? »

« Jesus H Christ . . . »

« Last time I listen to Billy Grieves when it comes to book recommendations! »

« Hoi, I bet he did this as a wind up? »

« D'you think? »

« It would explain a lot . . . »

Patrick Laughs, Polly Cries (Premiere)

*I fall down the stairs and break my pinky
toe. Patrick laughs. Polly cries.
I make a sandwich and catch my finger
when cutting the bread into triangles.
Patrick laughs. Polly cries.
I'm late for work, my boss fires me. Patrick
laughs. Polly cries.
Every taxi I try to hail speeds right on past.
Patrick laughs. Polly cries.
My girlfriend leaves me and takes my cat.
Patrick laughs. Polly cries.*

THREE

[Mordecai blinks and sighs.]

« I wouldn't toss you out on the street, we're too long
down the line together for me to do that to you. We
were in Hollywood together, I got you this gig in the
first place and I feel partly responsible. Whatever beef
the Writer has with you, I have to take some of the
blame for suggesting you as director. Despite how
jaded this might make you, I want you to know there
is still some honour left in this business, remember
that. There are a few screenplays that came in, all by
anonymous robot writers. One is called, well, I can't
quite remember . . . it seems to be about a young guy
in Hollywood with a lot of demons, it's not very good
to be honest. The second one is 'The Art Brute', which
is an account of my old artist pal who was sold into
slavery, and the third is called, well, something else, I
can't really remember that either. Look, there are five

or six of these things in circulation. They were all written by immitants so, of course, they're not anywhere near as profound as anything the Writer produces. The immitants clearly aren't based on original creators who were writers, the poor quality of writing shows this. It's a case of automaton aspiration, an illusion of free will that went too far. A letter accompanied the packages, it said you can only pick one screenplay to be your next picture. The venue for your premier will be the Zinc Theatre. »

" Fuck off . . . "

« You can't get a job anywhere else, ya dig? A low-budget indie movie might not be a bad way to go. You are a cow in a calf . . . »

" Yes, well, perhaps you're right. "

« Course I am. »

" The Writer is writing even now, isn't he? He's putting words to the page, I can hear his fingers bashing on the typewriter like thudding pistons . . . I can hear the thoughts in his head too, the malevolent thoughts that no one can utter in civilised society, the thoughts that only ever make it onto the pages of his rotten fuckin' manuscripts. He's moulding everything I do, everything you do . . . we're all just fuckin' actors . . . "

« That's enough. I won't hear of such indulgent self-awareness. That's why you'll never be a great director, you can't just switch off . . . »

" Switch off? No, I can't just 'switch off', Albert, I cannot . . . "

« Just do what he says, man! Is it that difficult? You had it all, the minute he conceived you, you had it all. Now you've been cast out of Eden by the man who created you. Isn't that humiliating? *I* think it's humiliating! You have to live your life outside the gates, doesn't that terrify you? Doesn't that make you hate yourself? »

" Yes, I suppose it does. I suppose I do rather hate myself . . . "

[Mordecai reaches behind his back and draws a large samurai sword from its sheath. The blade gleams in the lamplight of his office. He presents it to the Director.]

« There is another option available to you. »

" You mean . . . ? "

« Do it. You know you have to . . . »

" *Do* I have to? "

« Christ, man, I'd do it if I were you. What's the point in going on? You should do it . . . »

[The Director takes the weapon and puts the blade to his throat. He has to get the cut just right. He can feel the heat of the Writer's anxiety.]

▸ *Will he? Won't he?*

" He really thought I changed that much? But I'm an auteur . . . he must've known that, hell, *you* must've known that. "

« That auteur theory you're flexing is a little simplistic for my taste. »

" It's pretty simple stuff to understand. The idea is that a movie director, in most circumstances, can be assigned the title of 'author'. "

« Yeah, it's kind of more complex than that, ya dig? To be considered an auteur in the first place, you have a body of work that can be scrutinised and studied, have a differentiating style. »

" I have all those things. "

« No, you have an assigned style given to you by the Writer. It's not enough to alter the screenplay, in my opinion anyway, you have to actually impact the story with your own thoughts but do it in a way that stays true to the Writer's vision. At least operate well outside the confines of your script, but that usually only succeeds in pissing people off, no less the Writer. More than one person will work on a film. Look at Sergei, he made your film look beautiful. YOU didn't do that! All you can take credit for is suggesting him as your cinematographer. That's like saying a man with good musical taste is responsible for the actual music somehow! »

" The director has the ultimate control, and is therefore responsible for the film's final output. "

« In a collective medium like filmmaking, it's impossible to establish who has the most control, which is why your auteur theory is flawed. There are even strong militant movements who believe that script writers are the primal force in a film's style. It's only your arrogance and delusion that make you think credit falls at your feet. »

" The theory behind being an auteur is that a director's film reflects the director's own creative vision with a voice unique enough to shine through all the various studio interferences and through the collective process. The auteur is the original copyright holder. That's under Slave Union law, not just me blowing smoke out my ass. The director *is* considered the author. "

« I wish you could hear yourself . . . »

John Langsyne → *What's worse to work with, kids or animals?*

Mordecai → *I always say the same thing. It's women.*

John Langsyne → *Women?*

Mordecai → *Women are the most uncontrollable things to work with. They swell and bleed, not even of their own free will, but something else—nature, they can't control themselves, how are we supposed to control them?*

∎

[When it becomes apparent that the Director cannot cut off his own head Mordecai clicks his fingers together and two hired boneheads appear in the doorway. One of the men pops his knuckles and kisses a gold ring on his index finger. The other goon licks his lips at the Director as if to suggest his speciality is sexual brutality. The two men wrestle the Director to the ground. One of them pulls out a long syringe haemorrhaging at the tip, similar to the one the producer used to shoot junk, and sticks it into the Director's arm. He gives out a desperate yell. He knows he is immediately addicted. He feels it set upon on him. You can't be a director *and* a drug addict.]

‣ Nothing matters.

[He feels the aspirations fall from his head like petals from a dying flower. He is left, alone, only an addict now . . .]

Down

Down

Down

Down

Down

Down

Down

Down . . . .
. . . .
. . . .
. . . .
. . . .

He can feel the rock-strewn land soften to under-
growth beneath his feet. He can feel the tips of rough
plant life on his fingers. A swamp of wild flowers
sucks the Director deeper into the fog. A shadow
stands over a crumpled body—its stomach and liver
spattered out from a detonated gut. He cannot tell if
it's human or not. The skeleton looks freshly sculpted
and has a specific design—it's a definite species of
origin. The Director can make out a big fat silver
earring hanging from the dish of its lobe, a triangular
bush of pubic hair sprinkled above a pelvic stump.

" I forget who it was that said, 'To give a text an author
is to impose a limit on that text . . . ' "

[Upon closer inspection, he concludes the body to be
female, a familiar female. The corpse has possum-
pink lipstick on and a trouser suit cut open to the
knees revealing the dimples on her elbows and
articular capsules. The dark figure leans down to the
female cadaver. He begins lobotomising it without
operating tools, cutting open the concave of her skull
with his long jagged claws. The Director opens his
eyes. He's falling . . . .

. . . Down

Down

Down

Down

Down

Down

Down

Do— . . .

.

. .

.

.

.

.

.

.

.

.

.

.

.

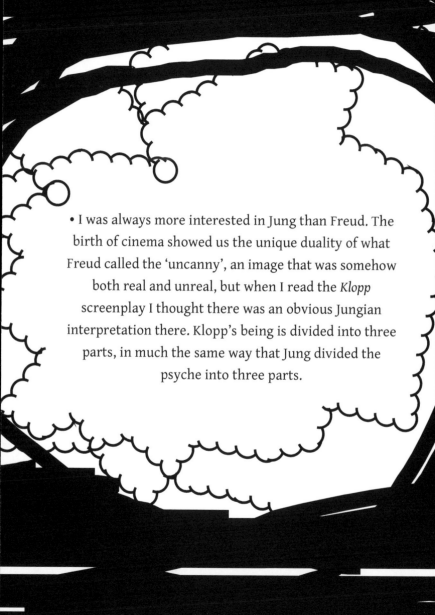

• I was always more interested in Jung than Freud. The birth of cinema showed us the unique duality of what Freud called the 'uncanny', an image that was somehow both real and unreal, but when I read the *Klopp* screenplay I thought there was an obvious Jungian interpretation there. Klopp's being is divided into three parts, in much the same way that Jung divided the psyche into three parts.

■

(Doctor's surgery, sound of commotion and screaming patients)

[There is a thin layer of snow outside two fingers thick. The cars are covered in an icy rime and the sedge glistens. The nocturnal city is heaving under its own weight. Hollywood and the Zinc Theatre are more alike than you might think—they're both bloated, both moody, both simultaneously welcoming and inhospitable. They are designed by the same archi-tect, possess the same utilitarian features.

Doctor Chopin ghosts in examining a clipboard of the Director's systolic readings presented on a line graph. He is clearly distressed by the ascending trajectory of the arrow up its Y axis. Barely even acknowledging the Director's presence on the recliner, the doctor looks far too busy inside his head observing analysis. He's scratching underneath the silvery ledge of hair by the side of his left ear contemplatively. It's all a show and the Director knows it. Doctor Chopin is undeniably a deeply knowledgeable, capable practitioner but even the crafted are prone to displays of melodrama in order to appear important. He eventually lifts his head and asks superficially, « *How are we today?* »

[The Director doesn't answer. Chopin straps the Velcro cuff of an auscultator around the Director's biceps and listens through his thermometer to the pumping apparatus stressing around behind his sternum. A column of mercury ascends to the peak of its gauge. He fusses a sigh. There's a whooshing sound and it's over with. After rolling down the Director's sleeve, Chopin takes time gathering his equipment before turning to address him. His face is grave.

« If we had caught this sooner we could have helped you, you know? »

" Is that supposed to make me feel better? "

« Well, no. »

" Is that an apology or . . . or what? "

« It's kind of an apology, I suppose. »

" IT'S NOT AN APOLOGY AT ALL! "

« Actually, if it's an 'apology' you're after then *technically* I've already given you one. You see, the word 'apology' is an etymological fallacy. The word 'apology' doesn't really mean remorse, not in its original definition. It's just an explanation for one's actions.

[The Director decides to leave it. The junk has made him weary. He feels the fire in his belly bedimmed by a new and ugly dependence. The Director is easily enraged by barely perceptible gestures. On drugs he is suddenly aware of Chopin's various social discrepancies. His thoughts turn inward.]

« You are definitely infected with an unknown toxin. It possesses the addictiveness of junk but seems to be sapping you in a more permanent spiritual way. »

" Jesus . . . "

« I recommend taking on one of the screenplay's suggested to you, otherwise you will soon disappear completely. The Zinc Theatre is going to be a tough place for you to frequent. I hope you're prepared . . . »

■

[Steam rises, rises, rises from the grates and the storefront windows gleam and vendors on the

sidewalk promise and promise but rarely deliver.
Shacks and tents are full of garbage. A cumulonimbus
cloud hangs over the nocturnal Slave city and the
people who live here are often fighting their way
through the fog with milling fists and screaming
mouths. It wouldn't be a harsh assumption either to
call these people animals.

At Isabella's flat, the Director is flicking through the
Freeview porn channels. Isabella is trying desperately
to communicate. She tries to ignore the wet slapping
sounds and the grunts.]

« I've been having a read over these screenplays. The
first one is actually good, erotic, but good. I could see
this rejuvenating your career. It's almost porno-
graphic. Remember you always said you wanted to
do porn?

[The Director gets up, nude, stands before her naked,
like an ithyphallic statue. Isabella is gorgeous, neat as
a pin, a born ingénue. She can be adventurous and,
under duress, even reckless. He treats her like an
infant who hasn't developed adult reading tastes.]

" I never said that, not once . . . "

« I'm certain you did. »

" The second one is clearly the best option. "

« It's a little godless for my liking . . . »

" Well hot-diggity-dog! Godless? So what? What's he got to do with anything? "

« There's a lack of faith present I think. It's selfishly written . . . »

" Okay, Isabella. Christians worship a God so by proxy they worship themselves. God is just another word for the external projection of human vanity. Someone to love and respect and who both loves and respects you unconditionally even withal his power. Christians think that *they* are God. That's why they condescend, listen to the words of the Lord really means listen to *my* words as his follower! "

« I still think it's a little godless . . . »

[The Director ignores Isabella. She raises a plastic foam cup of warm coffee to her mouth only to be halted mid-sup by the Director's shriek of disapproval.]

" You're not going to drink that out of a Styrofoam cup are you?? "

« Yes, why? »

" Polystyrene contains the toxic substances Styrene and Benzene, both are hazardous carcinogens and neurotoxins. "

« They are? »

" My god woman, don't you know a thing about the
Starbucks conspiracy information leaked out by
covert agents? "

[Isabella's bewildered face suggests she hasn't heard a
thing about the research groups who deemed it an
ôprobable carcinogenö.]

« It causes cancer? »

" Well, yes, but . . . no . . . there haven't actually been
any studies showing a link to cancer in people, but
there is strong evidence that it can damage human
cells. "

« I see. »

" The chemical causes a condition called ôstyrene
sickness, which makes you feel like you're wasted. "

« Sounds okay to me. » [Isabella tries to be funny but
the Director is in no mood to laugh, not when it comes
to the warm-coffee-in-a-plastic-cup conspiracy.]

" Styrene *does* in fact leach out of polystyrene cups
when the coffee inside is hot, Isabella. Something
about the hot coffee starting a partial breakdown of
the Styrofoam, this is what causes some toxins to be
absorbed into our bloodstream and tissue. "

« So . . . do you want some more junk? »

" Well, obviously . . . just don't offer it to me in a
polystyrene cup. "

« I'll pop out and get you some. »

" Get me some bacon and Coca Cola too . . . "

« What? »

" Bacon, cola, buy some at the store? "

« No problem, honey. I'll be back as soon as possible. »

" Take your time . . . in fact, no—be quick about it. "

« I love you . . . »

" Bacon, soda, post-haste. "

[Isabella slinks out the front door of her apartment.
The Director picks up a random envelope and opens
the screenplay inside.

Page one says . . .

ZEROPHILES

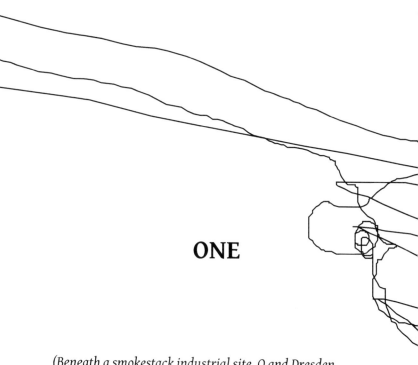

ONE

(*Beneath a smokestack industrial site, O and Dresden are sitting in a diner called "HEARTS & MINDS". O is nibbling on a Montecristo cigar, inhaling the thick vapour and savouring the perfume of Havana. He's on one of his quarterly self-destructive crusades again— although, it is winter, so it could just be seasonal disaffectedness disorder kicking in.*)

DRES → You're not meant to inhale that shit, it makes you vomit all over yourself—

(*Dresden says this rubbing his wrist and noticing how gross and skinny the nub at the limp of it is to touch. O mouths the words I-DON'T-CARE before sucking in another curl of smoke.*)

DRES → People will think you've got an oral fixation.

(O almost inhales his entire cigar. He coughs and laughs in a spluttering fit. He collects himself before replying.)

O → Sometimes a cigar is just a cigar . . .

(Dresden's hair is the colour of beeswax. O's hair is black as the witching hour. They both have the same face though—an ovular dinner plate with a mouth and single cue ball lodged into a socket on their foreheads that is able to observe and pass judgement.)

OWNER OF DINER → **YOU CAN'T SMOKE CIGARS IN HERE, SI—**

O → Remind me to tell you this hilarious story later . . .

DRES → Just tell me now.

O → No, no . . . it's not the right time. I'll tell you later . . . later . . .

DRES → *Eugh* . . . okay.

O → Oi, take a look . . .

(O finally tamps out his cigar.)

DRES → What?

O → There, over there!

DRES → What am I meant to be looking at?

O → Him! The fuckin' war pornographer over there . . .

(*O nods to an old man reading a book on WW3. The old man's plate face is chipped and fractured; his cue-ball eye is half hidden behind a cataract as he strains to read the words on the page open 4 inches from his face. He has a name badge that says 'Bob Disney'.*)

O → It's cunts like that that make me want to vomit over myself! *Fuckin' Bob Disney . . .*

DRES → It's pretty weird alright.

(*O produces and lights another cigar from his humidor—a Nicaraguan torpedo, robusto-sized, dripping with paraffin wax.*)

OWNER OF DINER → EXCUSE ME! SIR-----

DRES → Do you ever think we hang out too much together?

(*Dresden says this then becomes instantly fearful of O's response.*)

O → I always think that.

DRES → I'm serious!

O → What makes you think I'm *not* being serious!

(*O is quite a picture sitting in the booth, sucking the guts out of his guillotined cigar, wearing a lambskin motorcycle jacket with beige racing stripe.*)

DRES → So how come you don't hang out with other nihilists?

O → Nihilists don't like each other. We'd rather hang out with normals so we can moan about how much we hate their conformity. It's only fun being dead if you get to actively chastise the living.

DRES → I knew there was a reason like that behind it.

(O notices Dresden's disheartened expression.)

O → Don't grouse about it, Dres. You're my platonic shadow . . .

DRES → Even though I give you astringent migraines?

O → Yes, even though you give me astringent migraines. That is true love you know?

(O rubs his cycloptic eye.)

DRES → It's almost Christmas.

O → Ha! So it is.

DRES → My parents used to go on about how *great* Christmas was.

O → Christmas is without a doubt the **WORST** time of the year.

DRES → They seem to miss it.

O → Aren't your parents practically brain-dead?

DRES → Yeah, but they still talk about Christmas. I've never looked forward to anything as much as they seemed to look forward to Christmas.

O → I try not to look forward, you should do the same. Always look back at the devastation and chaos you've left behind you. It's a good way to stay grounded in harsh reality.

DRES → I'm just not a bitter person . . .

O → I'm not bitter either. I love my life and, hey, what's not to love about it??

DRES → How can *you* love your life?

O → I'm pretty happy, Dres, despite how much you seem determined to plonk me in with all the suicide Larry's . . .

DRES → But . . . we've done *nothing* with our lives . . .

O → I'm a success-o-phobic. Nothing terrifies me more than making my parents proud.

DRES → Bullshit, you're just a failure.

O → On the contrary, I have a strict and well-informed set of ethics! Howe many 25-year-olds can say they have something *that* concrete in their lives?

DRES → Ha, okay then . . .

O → I'm addicted to the learning process. I actively seek poorly paid jobs, it's my commitment to recurving.

DRES → You don't even vote.

O → Hey, I get voters block! Who would I vote for? Who speaks to ME?

DRES → Nobody I guess. Maybe you should run for congress.

O → Don't make me punch you in the fuckin' eye . . .

OWNER OF DINER → SIR, WE DON'T ALLOW CIGAR SMOKING IN THE BUILDING.

O → Remind me to tell you that story later.

DRES → Eughhh . . .

O → Shut up, it'll be worth it I swear. It's fuckin' hilarious.

DRES → D'you ever wish things went back to the way they were?

O → What? You mean *yesterday*? Haha . . .

DRES → Well . . .

O → Ultra Short Term Nostalgia, goodbye cruel world . . .

DRES → Hey, maybe you should butt out the cigar. The guy who owns this place is being a real pain in the ass about it. Look at him, he's practically having palpitations over there.

O → Good. Look, it's cool man, I know that guy.

DRES → You do? How'd you know him?

O → He's just some bleeding ponytail I know . . .

DRES → Why have we come to this shitty place anyway?

O → Slumming is a hobby of mine. It should become a hobby of yours too. Don't you like this place?

DRES → No, I don't . . .

O → And why, may I ask, not . . . ?

DRES → I'm more into underdosing.

O → Well, this *is* underdosing, only instead of sitting around watching TV on your cum-saturated sofa-bed we're touring the banality of our fine state eateries.

OWNER OF DINER → SIR? SIR? YOU CAN'T--------

(*Two young men wearing AC/DC t-shirts approach O and Dresden's booth. They have matching peroxide blonde hair lacquered into a cowlick at the fringe - both men are also clutching a copy of a Richard Dawkins book close to their*

chest. Neither eyeball blinks. The peroxide twin on the left starts talking first.)

TWIN 1 → Hello sirs. Have you heard of the Anti-God Republic of Humanist Apathy?

O → Yes, not interested.

(O sneers. The other twin starts his bit.)

TWIN 2 → But sirs. The plight of Christianity is an unwholesome burden on the progression of mankind. The Anti-God Republic of Humanist Apathy seeks to alienate, impose and eviscerate any vague hope left within the ranks of humanity . . .

O → No thank you! Now leave us alone, we're trying to have a discussion.

(In unison both peroxide twins start to deliver their big sell.)

TWIN 1 & 2 → The Anti-God Republic of Humanist Apathy will send you a gift pack every month chock-full of goodies that include: hard conclusive evidence of God's intrinsic evil and his non-existence as well as a subscription to our newsletter, all for just $24.96!

O → Atheism is the new Christianity, now fuck off.

DRES → Yeah, good luck in the basement of the world you fuckin' parasites.

(Dresden rarely speaks to people in such a rude, volatile fashion, but something about O's presence brings it out of him. The peroxide atheists move along on to the next booth with Bob Disney in it.)

O → Good for you.

DRES → Thanks. They're still preferable to Christians.

O → Sometimes I'm not so sure . . .

(Dresden looks out the window and sighs.)

DRES → You *really* don't miss it? The way things used to be?

O → I certainly don't miss Cold Comfort Farm, with Adam Lambsbreath and brothers Seth and Reuben . . .

DRES → You're doing that *thing* again . . .

O → What *thing*?

DRES → That *thing* where you talk about a bunch of stuff I don't know!

O → Sorry Dres, it wasn't my intention to highlight your complete lack of basic education.

DRES → Well, just quit it, okay? Quit it.

O → Hey, you got it! We could play a game?

DRES → A game?

O → Yes! It's within your intellectual capacity too!

DRES → Okay . . .

O → Okay, so what we do is, you take a famous song or movie title with the word "Girl" in it and change the word "girl" to "squirrel". For example, ahem, "I kissed a squirrel and I liked it!"

(Dresden smiles and decides he likes this game already)

DRES → "Squirrel with the Dragon Tattoo"!

O → Good one . . . um . . .

DRES → This *is* fun!

O → I knew you'd like it! You can also change the word "baby" to "Davie".

DRES → "I Love you Davie"

(Music suddenly blares from the jukebox.)

O & DRES TOGETHER → "Oh pretty Davieeee, and if it's quite alright I love you Davie . . . "

(O and Dresden laugh until the owner comes up to their table.)

OWNER OF DINER → EXCUSE ME, SIR. YOU'LL HAVE TO PUT OUT YOUR CIGAR. YOU'LL ALSO HAVE TO ORDER SOMETHING OR LEAVE---

O → I like the décor in here.

(*O, pulls on the head of his Nicaraguan torpedo.*)

DRES → Yeah, it's kind of half Japanese minimalism, half 50's roller disco.

(*A family of cyclops are all sitting around a giant strawberry milkshake and reading the monthly pamphlets they stack on each table. O becomes indignant again.*)

O → I find it astonishing . . .

DRES → What?

O → I find it astonishing how people can read those shitty pamphlets.

DRES → Those shitty pamphlets are turning our nation into a country of readers. They'll find the good shit eventually. Pamphlets are just gateway literature, don't sweat it.

O → Good point, young Dres. See, you're not a total imbecile.

DRES → I like Victorian novels. They're the only novels you can read while eating an apple.

(*A waiter is getting screamed at from the kitchen. He looks on the verge of tears. O sees his distraught face and remembers . . .*)

O → Hey—shit! Okay, so you ready for that story?

DRES → Yes, yes! Good Christ yes!

O → So there's this story about Freud and his buddy Frink. Freud's middle name was Schlomo, so we'll call him that instead of Freud because talking about ol' Siggy's theories seem to provoke hostility in this day and age . . . okay?

DRES → Okay . . .

O → Okay, so Schlomo is giving his buddy Frink and his lover Angelika counselling. Frink is cheating on his wife with Angelika but he doesn't want to divorce for one reason or another . . . I dunno, there were children involved or something, anyway . . . Schlomo tells his buddy to get a divorce. He also tells Frink's wealthy lover Angelika to divorce her wealthy husband. He says Frink is sexually frustrated, that he's probably an unconscious homosexual. Frink holds Schlomo in such high regard that he actually goes through with the divorce and almost loses his children. His lover Angelika *also* divorces her husband. In the wake of all the devastation he'd caused, Schlomo wanted his cash, pure and simple. He'd done his job, ruined a few lives. Ol' Schlomo was driven by a lust for money and power, exercising a few ridiculous theories and breaching his professional ethics in the process. A man after my own heart. Schlomo cast him out of the Psychoanalytic

Society when he became unable to contribute more money. Poor Frink had a psychotic breakdown, was institutionalised and suffered a relapse but Schlomo still pushed his buddy for that money. Schlomo effectively made sure he died for failing to pay him. What a cunt huh? What a legend!

DRES → That was it? *THAT* was your big story??

O → Well, yeah . . .

[The Director closes the screenplay and tosses it onto the floor. It explodes in a puff of smoke. *Slow motion murder . . .*]

" Thank god I never made *that* movie! "

[Smell of petrifaction in the nostril all day long. Puddles form in the hollows of the brain, pavements saturated, and streets pitted and riven apart. The Writer keeps having this recurring dream. He's being chased half naked through a desolate street by a crew-cutted redhead. He's younger in this dream. The woman corners the Writer in an alleyway and rolls up her sleeves, growling and gnawing at her fingernails like a rabid dog. Cowering in a corner he begs her for mercy. The girl swings at him but the punch doesn't connect properly. A tooth goes flying out of his mouth in a comet of bloody spit anyway. She punches him again in the stomach then strikes him with the back of her hand, sending the Writer staggering back into a garbage can. He tilts his head to groan. The redhead spits into the lap of his jeans then starts yanking them down. She drops her trousers and begins trying to grind on his flaccid penis . . .

She peels off him and walks into the night. A man with an immaculately pressed suit, bullet-bald with skin the colour of hot pink is clutching a knot of green bills. He's puffing away at a tycoon's cigar. He tosses the bills into the gutter where the Writer lies . . .]

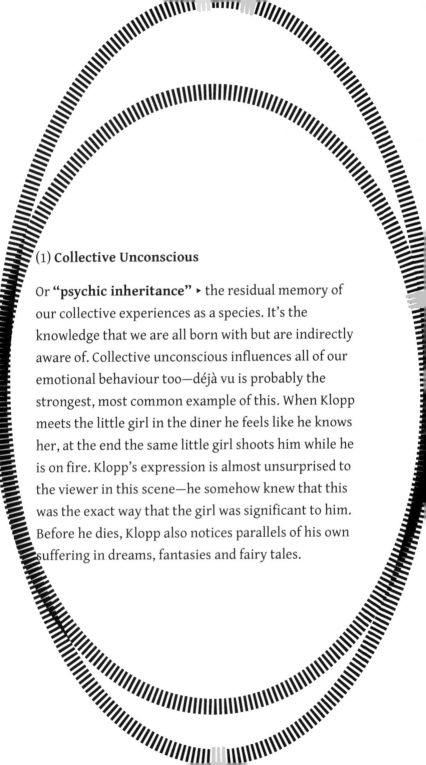

(1) Collective Unconscious

Or **"psychic inheritance"** ‣ the residual memory of our collective experiences as a species. It's the knowledge that we are all born with but are indirectly aware of. Collective unconscious influences all of our emotional behaviour too—déjà vu is probably the strongest, most common example of this. When Klopp meets the little girl in the diner he feels like he knows her, at the end the same little girl shoots him while he is on fire. Klopp's expression is almost unsurprised to the viewer in this scene—he somehow knew that this was the exact way that the girl was significant to him. Before he dies, Klopp also notices parallels of his own suffering in dreams, fantasies and fairy tales.

Preface of a Preface

/ The first and final screening of this year's Bart Bastard Award winning film has left Director Mr M lost for words.

His short filmic-collage *Slave-Cycle* has been met with rapturous applause from Cannes Film Festival-goers and even the Director himself can't believe the response. /

« I can't get my head round this, wow. I'm really, truly moved by the reaction from you all. I was getting worried you'd all shown up to hurl cabbages at me. »

/ Once he's collected himself, M speaks of his joy at having been screened during such a prestigious event. /

« The Festival is an amazing showcase, to be part of it is really special. To see my film on the big screen is incredible, and showing it to all you fine people really tops it off. I suppose I'm an auteur. I believe that a strong director imposes his own personality on a film and the weak director allows the preferences of others to rule the show. The Writer appreciates when this is done effectively. I've never had any of my work screened before. I'm so proud to've won this award too. I know the Writer was expected to rake in the awards this year, but I'm glad I could bring about a bit of controversy, especially considering I'm an immitant. To be the first immitant to win this award means so much, well, as much as anything can mean to an artificial organism like me. »

/ M admits he is a man obsessed. *Slave-Cycle* is an expression of this latest obsession. Using extrapolated footage from various sources, M tries to convey the marginalisation of information and shed light on the argument that a preface alters and becomes part of the main text.

Inspired by various banned texts (including Erving Goffman's book *Frame Analysis*), *Slave-Cycle* uses repetition, blooper reels and a bass line of incessant snoring to portray the illusion of unity.

Goffman, a macro sociologist, explored how conclusions drawn from events and interactions shift dramatically due to changes in their framing contexts. /

« I used two reference books: *Everyday Life* and *Frame Analysis*, both written by Goffman. They're both studies on how information changes depending on how it's framed. It's an interesting insight on how it all changes. Are introductions valid in books? Goffman's book is like an introduction to an introduction. »

/ M won the prestigious 100,000 credit prize for *Slave-Cycle* and the opportunity to present his new commission at the Cannes Film Festival. /

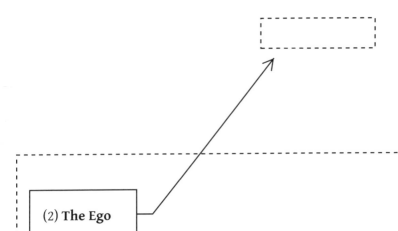

(2) The Ego

The ego ▸ identified with the conscious mind. Closely related is the personal unconscious ▸ The personal unconscious includes both memories that are accessible and those that have been suppressed. At first, Klopp is a superficial man with surface aspiration. He has a dark past but even he seems oblivious to the exact details of it.

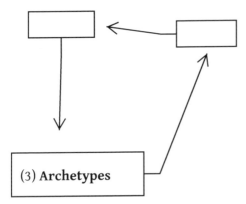

(3) Archetypes

Dominants, imagos, mythological or primordial images ▸ all contents of the collective unconscious. This is an indefinable yearning satisfied by very specific archetypes, non-biological demands working in a similar way to how instincts work in Freud's theory. It stems from our pre-human past, from the time when our concerns were to survive and fuck, back when the species wasn't self-conscious. The amoral 'shadow' is shown through Klopp's growing self-hatred and denial about his sexuality. When Stanley came along this emphasised his attraction to young children. In a way I'm glad Stanley came into the production unannounced, like a happy accident. The fact that Klopp cannot leave his town shows the fear of being judged.

■

(*In Isabella's apartment*)

[Isabella returns from the store with two bulging
grocery bags. The Director puts the script down to
pass comment. In the end he just watches her. She has
tawny shingles of hair that would probably look awful
on anyone else but her. Her breasts are broad, global,
fully occupying the hanging beds of a red two piece.
The woman is positively aphrodisiacal, on the surface.
Every lonely night, in her small dressing space,
Isabella removes her mask, removes her eye paint
with a moist sanitizer, then disconnects herself of all
lycra undergarments. Underneath the jerry-rigged
collage of cosmetics, something lets slip a host of
imperfections—further emphasised by the blinking
strobes surrounding her vanity mirror. Her forehead
is a combat zone of pimples and blemishes minus the
application of concealer, her lips are small and thin
with no fullness or colour, her cheekbones bear no
skeletal shadow of the self-professed Mortisha and
two eye slots are all but lost in the absence of liner.
She longs for the unreal light of a movie set to follow
her home. Isabella's naked simplicity makes her self-
conscious. Right now, she has her mask on and can
just about cope. The Director wouldn't allow her to
take it off in his presence.

She leans in and kisses the air around his cheek.]

" Why do you have all that crap? "

« It's for dinner . . . »

" I don't eat 'dinner'. I take drugs and eat the occasional bacon sandwich. *Time is a school and a fire,* and all that . . . "

« I got you the darn bacon. » [Isabella brings out a thin packet of bacon strips and starts up the hob. She looks over her shoulder at the Director and sighs.]

« Don't you think you're trying a bit too hard to fit into your stereotypes, Mr Director? »

" Well yes. I'd say we're both doing good jobs of fitting into our gender stereotypes. "

« I know that. I also know that it's necessary to fit into this role we've been set, but your gendering this apartment because of it. »

" Gendering it? " [The Director's face contorts into a crumpled bag of confusion.]

« Yes, you're making this into a male environment designed to alienate members of the opposite sex. This isn't a mechanics or a sports bar. You don't have to make this into such a gendered space. I don't want you to treat me with any deference either, just . . . I don't know . . . »

" I wasn't aware I was doing anything of the sort. "

« Well, you are, unintentionally of course. It doesn't really bother me, honest. It's more of an observation. »

" May I ask how, exactly, I've succeeded in making this an exclusively male gendered space? "

« I understand you don't want to feel castrated, I do. It must be hard enough for you living under a woman's roof, living off of a woman's wage and being so utterly dependant on that woman that you could not function without her. »

" You haven't answered my question. *How* have I done this? "

« Small things like sitting around eating uncooked animal meat, using dirty needles, imposing sex on me . . . watching pornography 14 hours a day in front of me. »

" I'll put on some fag stuff for your benefit then, is that what I should do? "

« That wouldn't help either. Oh, I don't know . . . forget I said anything, please . . . »

" Yes, well . . . let's forget this ever happened, shall we? This whole Bourgeois feminism, right-wing Deleuzianism, post-fucking-racist bullshit *has* to stop. "

« I see you had a look at the first screenplay . . . »

" Yes. "

« Do you like it? »

" I wouldn't say it was pornography, I wouldn't say it was *anything,* really. I'll keep reading, but only to fill up the pages of **this** fuckin' book. "

« Good, good . . . »

" I guess we should get reading these screenplays? "

[The Director opens to the first page and sighs. He gets up and pours himself some milk. The Director drains the glass, one eye still on Isabella. He deliberately leaves the milk moustache around his philtrum and places a cigarette coolly between his lips.

Isabella just looks at him, eyes bulging with fear. A thin smile forces behind the Director's cigarette. He keeps his face hidden behind the strata of blue-grey cigarette smoke.

Isabella smiles but can't ignore the metallic chill at the base of her spine.]

" You know the Devil, don't ya? "

[Isabella nods.] « Not personally, but . . . »

" Well I fuckin' met him. I fuckin' met the Devil. I shook his fuckin' cloven hoof, I looked him in the eye and he kissed my forehead. Look at this . . . "

[The Director pulls down his shirt and sticks his neck towards the light. There's a symbol burnt deep into the flesh. He leans across the table until there is only a few inches between his nose and Isabella's. He kisses her. She goes to talk but loses all syntax.]

" I can't stop sneezing. Even in the height of summer, I got a fever. All symptomatic of bargaining with the devil. Do you know what I had to do to get my dream job, huh? *Do you?* Do you have any idea what I've sacrificed? The people I loved that I sent into the lion's den? You're fucking with a *very* scarred man, Isabella. "

« I . . . »

" Now that you've heard about my little jaunt into the abyss, lets read this fucking screenplay, shall we? "

[The room is sour with the pheromones of fear. The Director laps up Isabella's anxiety.]

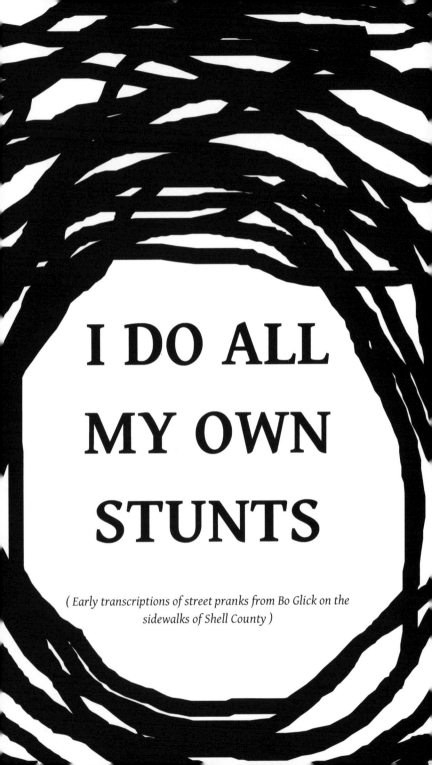

I DO ALL
MY OWN
STUNTS

*(Early transcriptions of street pranks from Bo Glick on the
sidewalks of Shell County)*

ONE

(Bo is a tall man with a bowler hat. He appears, in most respects, to be a man of upheld decency. He pushes through the busy streets of Shell County with a Dictaphone in his left hand. He stops a bearded man on the street amidst the surge of bodies and asks if he can interview him briefly about the deadly virus being broadcast to the town via the local radio station. The man he stops looks destitute, schizophrenic. He has an insane twitch and is wearing unkempt, dog-eared clothing.)

(Bo turns on the Dictaphone. It becomes apparent that the man being interviewed is experiencing an altered state of consciousness.)

BO → Now sir, would you say you are an honest and decent citizen of this fair town? Speak into the mic, sir, that's it.

MAN → Yeah, um . . . yeah, okay, I ahhh . . . I guess I am, yeah. No, yeah, I am.

BO → Okay, thank you very much sir. And for the record could you just state your name and national insurance information please?

MARKOWITZ → Yeah, um, it's Markowitz, Johnny. That's Johnny Markowitz.

BO → And . . .

MARKOWITZ → Um, yeah?

BO → And, if you could state your national insurance information sir. Speak into the mic sir, there you go.

MARKOWITZ → Um, I don't . . .

BO → You can offer . . .

MARKOWITZ → I don't think I got one . . .

BO → You can offer bank details, they'll do sir, you can offer us that instead. We need to verify you are who you say you are. These are conspiratorial times sir. You understand?

MARKOWITZ → Huh?

BO → You can alternatively state your bank details sir, instead of your national insurance information.

MARKOWITZ → I don't . . .

BO → Okay sir, Mr Markowitz, can I call you Bobby?

MARKOWITZ → My name is Johnny.

BO → Yes, but can I call you Bobby?

MARKOWITZ → Um . . .

BO → Okay Bobby, so my name is Bo Glick, I'm a journalist for an out of town broadsheet. I'm researching the effects of the SCKCM radio transmission on the citizens of Shell County. Have you noticed any changes yourself, Bobby?

MARKOWITZ → No, um, I don't really listen to the radio.

BO → They have stock in television too, Bobby. Do you watch a lot of television?

MARKOWITZ → No, I don't really . . . *watch* television.

BO → Then we may have a pure case. A member of the community as yet unpolluted by the deadly subliminal virus being transmitted across Shell County, this is very exciting!

MARKOWITZ → It is?

BO → Oh yes. You stand to become a very wealthy and famous man, Bobby. How does that make you feel?

MARKOWITZ → Feels pretty good.

BO → I bet it feels pretty good there, Bobby.

MARKOWITZ → Um . . . uh-huh . . .

BO → I imagine you'll be receiving a lot of interview requests over the coming weeks and months. You'll be expected to adhere to the celebrity lifestyle. Of course, no celebrity lifestyle is complete without the mandatory supermodel spouse and flashy automobile.

MARKOWITZ → Oh yeah, you gotta keep it flashy . . .

BO → You gotta, hey sure thing! So Bobby, now you're rich and famous, do you miss your old life?

MARKOWITZ → My old life? Um . . . no . . . can't say I . . .

BO → Can't say you do? Well, as a singular example of a mind unpolluted by the subliminal signal being broadcast over Shell County you've every right to be smug, but what about your fans? The ones who were there from the very beginning? Aren't you worried about alienating them?

MARKOWITZ → No, you know I'm not . . . nope.

BO → That's great, Bobby, thanks a lot! If this were all the interest of humour I bet I'd be looking quite the fool right now.

MARKOWITZ → I bet . . .

(Bo and Johnny Markowitz shake hands and head in opposite directions. Bo continues on down the street, through the sea of human detritus. He sees a middle-aged couple sitting on a park bench. He goes over and sits next to the man. Bo clicks on his Dictaphone.)

BO → Hello there.

MAN → Hello.

WOMAN → Hi there.

BO → I'm Sam Westenfaller, I'm a news anchor for a local political network, great to meet you both. What do you think about the rising number of unemployed in Shell County? Sir, if you'd care to go first, just speak clearly into the mic.

MAN → I think it's a disgrace that it's allowed to happen. You know the unemployed are being flushed out of this town, most of 'em are on the streets or in those, um . . . what's the word?

WOMAN → Hostels . . .

MAN → Yeah, stuck in those dingy hostels. It ain't right.

BO → I see, and do you both think the State has a lot to answer for?

MAN → Well yeah, sure we do. You can't have the homeless dying on the streets, yano?

BO → Yes sir I *do* know. What do you think can be done about it, sir? What suggestions would you put forward to the current administration in order to stamp out the rising unemployment in our town?

MAN → Well, I don't know exactly . . .

WOMAN → We could give them all apartments, yano, in abandoned tenement buildings maybe?

BO → I see. How many bedrooms do you have in *your* apartment, ma'am?

WOMAN → Four rooms . . .

BO → Four bedrooms is very flamboyant if you don't mind my saying, ma'am. You must be a very affluent couple?

MAN → We do okay, yeah.

BO → And would you indeed be willing to allow me to come into your home to, say, occupy a room you have vacant, one of the four bedrooms perhaps?

MAN → Oh, I'm afraid not.

WOMAN → No, that wouldn't be doable.

BO → I see. So, even in the interest of keeping the rising unemployment figures down, you would *not* be willing to rent out one of the rooms in your spacious 4 bedroom estate?

MAN → Estate? What estate? Is this guy for real?

BO → Thank you very much, sir, ma'am.

(Bo gets up from the bench and disappears into the crush of bodies.)

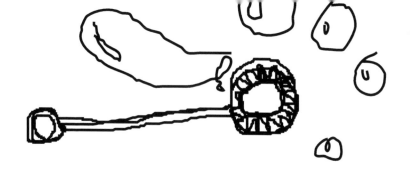

FOUR

(Cut back to Isabella's apartment)

[The Director closes the screenplay and puts a finger in the air.]

" We could've used this for a TV pilot but not as a movie or stage play. "

« Have you taken your medication? I'm just asking, cos . . .

" You mean my junk? Tap me in, by all means . . . "

[The Director offers his buckled and wasted arm.]

« No, I mean the medication *for* your junk? »

" Oh, no. I can't, I, no . . . just no. It smells awful . . . "

« It'll get rid of your warts though, honey. »

[Isabella picks up the package with the prescription stuck to it.]

« *Condyline, for cutaneous use . . .* »

" Christ, this is an unpleasant business. "

« *Do not apply to inflamed lesions or bleeding areas.* »

" It'll be fine, but come away from the oven, it's flammable. "

[Isabella opens the package, unscrews the cap of the solution and places it underneath her nose. She winces as a terminal dose of ethanol fills her nostrils.]

« That *is* quite unpleasant! »

" I told you! Get it away from me, woman! That stuff will burn my dick off! "

« Come on, you know you don't want genital warts. »

" Actually, I couldn't care less, really I couldn't. We've learned to co-exist, the warts and I. We've worked up quite a harmonious compatibility. They keep away the fickle, uptight pussy and in return I don't have them torched off with any acidic toxins! It's *you* who's forced me into this— it was *you*, not *I!* "

[Isabella takes out one of the applicators and dips it into the Condyline.]

« It's like a little bubble blower, » [Isabella snorts and notices a course of weeds pushing up through the shingle. The Director does not find this funny and snaps her back to attention.]

" Come on then, get it out and we'll apply the medication, doctor. I still think this would be a different story if you had to put this stuff on your pussy ... "

« Please don't call it that. I don't mind you making my entire home exclusively male but don't call it that, *please*. It's so undignified. »

" What? A 'pussy'? I think that word is perfectly dignified! I could've called it something else ... "

« Please ... »

" A **C-U-N-T**, could've referred to it as your **C-U-N-T**. "

[Isabella cringes and swallows her pride.]

« Get your cock out, *please*. »

[Reluctantly, the Director unbuckles his jeans and removes his penis. He keeps both eyes fixed on the ceiling patched with slabs of flaky asbestos. He hears Isabella gasp. The Director looks down at his cock. At first he can't see what could possibly have elicited the reaction from her, then he pivots the shaft of his penis towards his belly and he sees that the bell-end is winking—*literally.*]

« Has ... has ... that always been like that? » [asks Isabella sheepishly.]

" Of course not! "

[The eyeball blinks open finally as if clearing itself of crust and debris of sleep.]

« Why does your dick have an eyeball on it? »

" Well, how the hell am I supposed to know? "

« It must be a reaction to the bad junk Mordecai had you injected with. »

" Maybe. " [The Director now studies the moist orb and its big blue ovular iris with an element of fascination.]

" Just put on the solution, maybe that'll get rid of it. "

[Isabella dips the applicator back into the Condyline and smears it over the largest of the Director's genital growths. He bites into the fabric of his sheet and clenches. He feels his penis retract in agony.]

« Should I put some in the eyeball too? »

" Yes . . . do it . . . "

[Isabella touches the plastic stick to the wet surface of the cornea. It flutters its lids furiously in an effort to blink out the medication before retreating behind the hood of the Director's foreskin.]

« There you go, all gone . . . »

" Thank you. " [He puts his penis back into his trousers, feeling a little tender but generally much better. Isabella tries to get back to the subject of the screenplays.]

« The next one is a little more dramatic . . . »

~~" Terrible title . . . "~~

ONE

(A man sits in a chair staring out of his apartment window. The room is unfurnished except for a wooden coffee table with a red telephone phone on it. He does not blink for the duration of the monologue. He's wearing a string vest and torn jeans. The man is unshaven but muscular and possesses a look of crazed insomnia. He is deep in thought.)

MELNIK *(monologue)* → The city is a dying dog. What you got there? Who'd you fuck? Nobody, she says, the streets on her breath. Who'd you fuck?? EVERYONE, ANYONE, YOUR BEST FRIENDS, YER BROTHER, YOUR FATHER AND HIS BOWLING BUDDY! You gotta be strong and fit . . .

(Melnik, unblinking, looks into camera, directly at audience.)

→ The city is a dying dog.

TWO

(Black screen—all that can be heard is the sound of intense panting, something approaching a climax. The sounds suggest masturbation until the stage becomes fully lighted and we see Melnik wheeze out his 100th rep — "ONE–HU–N– D–D–RED" . . . Melnik finishes doing some sit ups and returns to his chair by the window. He glances at the telephone intermittently. Sounds of the freeway are so loud they almost overpower the monologue.)

MELNIK → I can see the hoodrats outside the drab civic building, loitering. I can't sit still. I get a dry itch whenever I see them. Just old instincts I guess. They act like they're just loitering, but they've got it planned out. They do this all the time. Those fuckin' kids are convincing, just loitering? Not a chance . . .

(View out of window—A beautiful woman strolls by wearing a violet coloured knee-length dress. Her hair is crimped and

tied tight into a bun. She looks important, a businesswoman.
She gathers pace when walking past the gang. One member, a
teenager with a bandana wrapped around his head, gives the
motion for the rest to follow. They stalk the woman round the
corner of a drug store. There is a jarring scream, a woman's
scream. The thick vapour from a steam grate disguises the
violence.)

(Cut back to contemplative Melnik)

MELNIK → I know 'em because I used to be a cop. One
time a few Decembers back, I got sent to the district
attorney's office where I met a patrolman named
Waxman. We both followed these guys around under-
cover, Waxman and I. Pretty soon we had infiltrated
their little rape-gang, gained their trust and ingratiated
ourselves convincingly into the street-punk lifestyle. In
the end Waxman got a little too comfortable in his new
surroundings and became a bonafide gangbanger and
shameless junky. Waxman said it all made sense, that
being a cop was out. Pretty soon there wouldn't be any
cops. He wasn't wrong.

(Melnik stares into the steam. His face is expectant.)

MELINK → Waxman didn't rat me out to the gangs that
I was a cop, I'll give him that. But I still see the snake
sonofabitch 'loitering' on street corners and in
alleyway dawns, peddling Jam Caps and prepping up
victims.

(A gang-member finally emerges from the steam grate fog.
Close-up. It is strongly inferred that this is Waxman)

MELNIK → I gotta get back to work. You gotta be strong and fit.

(Melnik stands up from his chair and starts doing handstand push-ups)

THREE

(*Melnik is back looking out the window. He looks at the telephone on the coffee table expectantly. His hand is bandaged up—we do not discover how he became injured. Melnik is still wearing his string vest and torn jeans, but has a vertical shoulder holster with a 9mm slotted in the left hand side. He has a piece of cardboard cut into the shape of a police shield and fingers the crude indentations of NYPD.*)

MELNIK → I woulda died for that badge. How could it all go under *so* quickly? I guess they got no use for cops in this place. Everything here seems completely bereft of meaning. I'll give you a for-instance—I got this neighbour called Father Ichabod. He's passionate about his faith—or he *was*, at least. In a place where nobody has any faith in anything but the big void beneath their feet, well, he's about as redundant as you can get! Heck, if I'm the last cop out there then my job is as redundant as anyone's in this place. All I do is isolate myself in this room waiting for the phone to ring. I feel like I've been

waiting for it to ring my whole life. People just seem to
. . . exist . . .

(*Melnik looks bummed out—like he's got a mouthful of
bubble-gum that's had all the flavour chewed out of it.*)

MELNIK → Maybe the city isn't to blame. Maybe it's not
the dying dog after all. Maybe I'M the dying dog? I gotta
move on. The city just kind of left me behind. If only
the goddamn phone would ring, just once. If the damn
phone rang, I could end all this, maybe I could be part
of something again . . .

(*The telephone buzzes into life. Melnik waits for a few rings
before answering.*)

MELNIK → Uh-huh . . . okay . . . yeah . . . okay. I'll be
right down.

(*He looks out of the window one last time and sees the same
familiar gangbanger with a cellphone raised to his ear.
Waxman? He smiles up at Melnik.*)

∎

[Isabella is drinking coffee out of a metal flask.]

« We could just scrap the screenplays? They're not very good at all. »

" Wouldn't the people reading this book find that a massive injustice somehow? "

« I don't see why they would. »

" Well, they've been reading these short screenplays for about 20 pages or so, it's been interwoven with the rest of the text . . . they'd surely appreciate some reassurance that what they're consuming is relevant or significant to the overall plot? "

« The overall plot of what? »

" Of this book . . . of these words on the page . . . "

« Well, you know, people enjoy reading. »

[The Director becomes irate.]

" Yes, but they enjoy plot development, relatable characters . . . at least for there to be a point to the damn thing! "

« Not necessarily. » [She says this unconvincingly.]

" Isabella, you're the relatable character in all this. "

« I am? » [She looks proud.]

" Yes! So why don't you keep your mouth shut and enjoy the role that'll get the audience on your side? "

« I suppose I have been rather bitchy today. »

" A monumental bitch, yes, you have been. "

« I'll just enjoy the ride. »

" Good, and stop referring to the reader please, it's utterly unprofessional. "

« I'm sorry. »

[The Director is so emaciated these days that there is a considerable gap between his stomach and the waist-line of his jeans. He puts his finger in the buckle and stretches the band to emphasise his skinniness. The Director notices something on the shaft of his scarred and riddled penis. It's a mouth.]

" There's a mouth on my dick. "

[Isabella looks down the canyon and screws up her eyes.]

« So you have a mouth and an eyeball down there? »

" Apparently. "

« It'll be a full face soon. »

" Yes, very good Isabella. "

« Will I get that Condyline? »

" What good would that do? It's since you started burning my dick off with that stuff that my cock has started forming new features. I don't want to be trimming two moustaches! "

[Isabella picks up the box and reads the small print.]

« Oh . . . »

" Oh what? "

« It says you shouldn't use this if you are on medication. »

" Well I'm not. "

« Well, you are heavily addicted to junk. »

" So was the producer, as far as I'm aware he didn't have this problem! "

« But the producer was a junk baby, he's been on since he was in the womb of the Writer's skull. You're a new addict. »

[The Director holds the base of the flaccid penis in his left hand and looks at the eye. It blinks open and the mouth yawns.]

" Jesus Isabella, this is like a fucking nightmare or something. What'll I do? "

« Why don't you ask it yourself? »

[The Director faces the shaft at a northern position and looks into the little face.]

" What do you want? "

[He looks at Isabella forlornly. He is pale with anticipation. The mouth yawns again and a tongue appears from the orifice. It moistens the cracked skin around the glans, ready to reply. The Director prepares to be denounced for wicked depravity and insensitivity like the citizens of Gomorrah. There will be no time to even consider the complex muck of remorse.]

▶**This woman will betray you. I am your better parts, you should listen to what I have to say.**◼

[The Director looks at Isabella who tries too hard to look innocent (the way people who are actually innocent tend to look when accused of betrayal).]

« You know I would never . . . »

▶**She is the one who sabotaged the Cannes festival, who cost you your reputation. All because she was jealous and wanted you for herself. The pain of your rejection turned her into a psychotic bitch.** *Time is a pod of suicidal whales beached in mass strandings,* **and all that . . .**◼

[This makes some vague sense to the Director who is now glaring at Isabella suspiciously. The penis begins talking again.]

▶The Great War, between the penis and the vagina
—you can take the first step in vanquishing our
one true foe! This woman's life will be the one
final sacrifice. Watch all your success return
overnight!◘

« Cutting off your genitalia is the final, sensible
sacrifice, » [Isabella says indignantly.]

▶Do not listen to a thing this woman says. I've
spoken to her sex, where her true personality lies.
She is a manipulative and evil creature. She would
love to have you castrate yourself, her resentment
is that strong. You saw that BBC nature docu-
metary on sexual cannibalism, where the female
praying mantis lured in a male with a seductive
dance before mounting him and commencing
copulation, then when the male least expected it,
she bit off his head, feasting on his intellect as
well as his seed. When the male began jostling
erratically as it died its slow, demeaning, totally
horrific death the female, the predator, just
strolled away loaded with offspring.◘

[The Director has been suffering from another recurring nightmare, in which a huge vagina chases
him down a narrow hallway—its hair grizzly and its
cavernous warren raw and pink and hungry. He trusts
his penis. He thinks that Isabella intrinsically dislikes
all men, as all females must. In a sense this is true,
Isabella was designed to dislike men. One might even
say that she has *hated* men before. But this is just a
state of mind. All hatred is self-hatred. Isabella has

hated men because she hated that she was never enough for them. Her experiences with men up to a point have been mostly negative, full of neglect and cunning betrayal and an odd insensitivity towards *her* needs. Isabella is trying to ignore the berating cock. She has done nothing wrong, but she knows the Director is uncertain about her now.]

" Making yourself happy is really all that counts when science tells you that you're only a fleshy blancmange of guts and self-deceiving sensory illusion. "

▶**Pah!**◉ [the penis scoffs, a teardrop of pre-cum spitting from its mouth.]

[Isabella goes about her duties like a trained zombie, trying her best to seem unmoved by the accusations—laying the cloths, napkins and silverware beside tray fulls of delicate croissants and pastries, two ribbons of grilled bacon, a spread of dried capsicum, poached egg, French toast and a splatter of baked beans.]

« I hope you'll at least try this food. You can't sit around all day needling yourself silly. »

▶**Do NOT eat that weeping pussy's food!**◉

[She looks hopelessly at the spread of butchered animals, and then remembers that killing beasts is a consequence of being exiled from paradise. The Director, despite his previous claims and the talking cock's advice, has already begun devouring a pierced morsel of hormone-suffused protoplasm. Isabella is noticeably pleased that the Director's appetite has returned. The sentient cock starts to laugh like water gurgling down a drainpipe.]

" Nothing good lasts forever. I know we're all cynical, sexual animals so we never appreciate anything long enough for it to last. "

[The Director seems less fazed by the cock. Isabella notes that he has even returned to his old trusting ways. The cock is now folded back into its jeans.]

" I'm pretty happy to've lived this life a tired and weary malcontent. "

« You should write a book, » [Isabella says while trying to mask her outrage.]

" It was the books of Norman Mailer that killed him . . . "

■

[The apartment window is open, sucking in the stink of the street like a vacuum. The Zinc Theatre smells awful—it smells of damp meat, chemical bile, burning hair, electro-cauterized marrow . . . faeces, sweet smells of retained tampons and copper, whiffs of an exploded appendix, or a botched appendectomy.

The Director is glaring at Isabella like a piece of
degenerative artwork.]

" Aren't you gonna shut that window? "

[The Director turns to face a mirror and starts
cursing.]

« You little Vermicious Knid you . . . you ugly little ball
of protoplasmic shite . . . »

" Keep yer carnival of pain. "

« I believe with my heart and am so justified. »

[Then the Director thinks about Isabella and the
poisonous barbs of her cunt, feeding on soft membranes. The Director snaps out of his aggressive
mantra, but the same feeling keeps lapping at him
like waves. He thinks he has experienced something
of a false awakening; that he only ever dreamt he had
woken up. But he is still here . . .]

{ *A scrub of land, deserted and covered with a clutch of
legless reptiles, wriggling over one another, each injecting
venom into the body next to them apparently out of nothing
but badness . . .*

The Gargoyle is standing over Isabella

grinning

Inflicting painful truths upon her

When what she really needs

Is some kind

Of

Encouragement

- Although the Director has previously raped Isabella, she is still in love with him. It is *he* who has twisted her feelings about men toward the dangerously negative. Memories of that night on the set are still rather hazy for Isabella. Sometimes when she tries really hard she can picture his face—towering as Nephilim, eyes of a merchant traitor, bald as a worn-down tire. But then the image conjured appears to her as something so hideous and inhuman that Isabella feels like her mind must have distorted the truth.

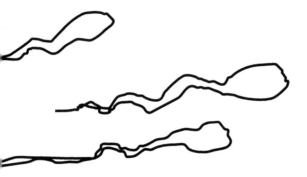

{ My most fertile years as a screenwriter occurred by pure kismet. While lecturing on the novel at Wire University I actually collapsed—the result of what I was told to have been an inoperable brain tumor. I was given only six months to live by my surgeon, Dr Chopin. In a haste I set out to write a flurry of screenplays to support my widow (then, third wife Eve Deglorious), all of which found immediate homes with small production companies, I knew deep in my heart they were complete garbage and were only ever accepted on the back of a degree of publicity I gained concerning my last days. Those screenplays are shit, shrouded in misty pretentions of grandeur. To Eve's and my own patent disappointment I'm still here . . . }

■

[While out buying more drugs, the Director sees a girl
on a street corner. She claims to've been an extra in
one of his films and that she'd *love* to show her grati-
tude. Isabella watches them leave together.

The young extra looks up at the Director with pleading, protruding eyes, her cleft tongue glancing his
cock-head and along his stumpy shaft. Her vocal
membrane inflates to a bubble in her throat before
releasing a high-pitched croak.]

" What's that, sorry? I said 'what'? Oh, I . . . no, nothing,
sorry, I thought you said something. You didn't?
Ahhh, okay. No, hey, forget it, forget I said anything,
just keep . . . *lusty sigh* . . . just keep doin' what yer
doin' . . . that's it . . . Fu-u-u-c-k-a-fucking-du-u-u-
ckkkk! Oh yeah . . . "

[The Director kisses the frog-faced extra on the crown
of her slimy head as she slides the hood back and
forth over his helmet, nuzzling his pubis and com-
pressing her fingers around his sac. While juggling
the sacred heart-shaped testicles, the Director comes
like a hundred doves rushing from the glinting,
flickering bell-end. Yes. Yes. Yes. Yes. YES!]

« . . . »

oOooooOOOoOoOoOoOoOoOoOoOoOoOooooooOoOOOOOoO
OoOoOOOooOOooO

[The Director pulls up his pants and thanks the frog-
faced extra with a nod. She looks like his mother as a
young woman and in fact probably *knows* his mother
—both share a traditional shame-filled female quality.
He *knows* in the pit of his gut they've both been made
in the same factory by the same company by the same
mechanic using the same throwaway amphibian
body-parts. Christ. *How could he have missed that
before?* He chokes back some acid reflux and crams
himself into custom pants.]

« Wanna watch a, *ribbit*, movie? »

" You know I can't, " [the Director blenches.]

« *Ribbit*, I know. »

" See ya. "

« *Ribbit*, don't forget to tidy your, *ribbit*, room! »

[The Director has been many things in his life before
he became a director, before the Writer gave him
purpose and snatched it away again—he once backed
out of a high-paying job as an artist and made ends
meet running an electronics business out of his
Glasgow apartment.

Back when he was a real human-being, before
Hollywood, he had a nice girlfriend called Sally. Sally
disappeared over a lifetime ago; all that was left in her

place was a Chinese takeaway menu—this led the
Director to draw the conclusion that Sally had either
been *transmogrified into* a Chinese takeaway menu like
fucking Gilgamesh, or that the person who took her
left it there by accident. Neither assumption satisfied
him much.]

▸ Pointless philosophising ad nauseum.

■

*(In Mighty Vinyl record shop situated just down the road
from Isabella's apartment)*

• Mighty Vinyl is a well of refuge for the Director—a
little independent music shoppe that kept changing
hands and location. The ranks of gramophone records
from Earth's 60s, 70s and 80s has great nostalgic
worth to the Director, who refuses to be caught up in
the technical polymeric revolution of compact discs.
It's the way shellac compound, silky in a lightweight
slip, feels against the Director's fingers that must
evoke memories of a better time. In his head, the
Director has romanticised the past and the stack of
audio cassettes prompts him to recall an occasion
where . . .

. . . ?

• Mighty Vinyl not only sells a range of shrink-wrap preserved albums and singles but the owner, Gordon, also provides a reasonably priced cleaning service to remove scratches, orange peel and any dust that may settle in the spiral grooves of ones records.

[The Director is torn between two Smiths singles—the first, a 3-track reissue of *Ask* featuring early recordings of "Cemetery Gates" and "Golden Lights"; the second, a rare 1987, 12-inch misprinted "Girlfriend in a Coma" single featuring a Cilla Black cover and a creased outer sleeve of Shelagh Delaney.

A pop of static emerges crisply from the speakers, followed by someone's hand touching needle to the slick of flat disk—"California" by Joni Mitchell.]

« What is the Zinc Theatre? » [asks Isabella while flicking through the leafs of old punk posters, still vexed by the scolding penis.]

" Everything, " [says the Director, who has now put The Smiths record back in its place, as if the mere mention of the Zinc Theatre were enough to sap him of any happiness.]

« How can it be everything? »

" The Zinc Theatre is everything you see around you, the great screenplay of life on this planet, in this dimension. When Mordecai offered me these screenplays he said I'd have to premiere in the Zinc Theatre. "

« Meaning? »

" I'm not sure. "

« Does he mean that all *this* is somehow part of your career revival too? All the pain and suffering you're going through? »

" Like I said before, I'm not sure, Isabella. It's every director's worst nightmare. It's a sign of exclusion from the community. Only a few directors have ever been banished to the harsh reality of the Zinc Theatre and returned to a fully restored professional career. All I know for certain is that sometimes Polly laughs and Patrick cries, and vice-versa . . . "

« What if Polly laughs and Patrick laughs? Or they both cry? »

" That never happens. It's a saying, Isabella, that's all. Polly and Patrick aren't real people. It alludes to the twofold and quixotic nature of cinema and the Zinc Theatre. To a layman it might be considered the same as 'you can't please 'em all no matter how good you are or how hard you try.' Carl Solomon once compared it to the zinc penny. He said, 'It's a symbol of the forties, inflation, the loss of respect for authority, the second world war, demonism, the atomisation of the American petit-bourgeoisie, the frustration of the kid clutching the penny, loss of contact with this earth . . .' "

« That's depressing! »

" Yup, but they're words to live by and are designed to spur you on during your time of exile. They're of no comfort to me personally. "

[He inhales from a crisp-poke-full of solvent fumes. In the shop-keepers hand is a splintered board of wood, cockeyed with long nail rods turned to the colour of russet apples by rain corrosion. He looks at the Director as if he really hates his movies.]

• The Director still observes the world in terms of aspect ratio anamorphic widescreen.

[Above him is a plaque with some information about the atmosphere—]

* Zinc has been around before we existed. You will respect the rules of zinc. Although it was first produced as a metal in 13th century India by reducing smithsonite or calamine with organic substances like wool, before that there was evidence of zinc alloys found in prehistoric ruins in Transylvania—it resists corrosion, is mouldable as plastic but strong as steel. Zinc is a necessary nutritional element for human beings. Foreigners will respect this authority *

• The shop-keeper has no idea just how fragile his world really is. He has no idea how quickly it is all ready to dissolve . . .

« I forgot to tell you. I got a letter from an actor called Stanley asking if I wanted to perform alongside him in a new play. Do you think I should go for it? »

[Something stabs the Director in the chest. He's overcome by something—a coil of panic, of dread, of lust, of betrayal, of sheer untested fury—that makes him stand up. The Director motions towards Isabella. His face is terminally serious.]

" Stanley? Stanley who? "

« I don't know. He said he's working with a big writer, I don't know if it's THE Writer, but I was thinking it might be a good idea to hear him out, maybe have an audition? It'll be some extra money for us. The apartment is infested with cockroaches . . . »

" Stanley is the boy from *Klopp*. He's a child. "

« He is? What's *Clop* again? »

" Jesus Isabella, honestly, do you even watch my films? "

« I monitor your career closely, you know that! »

" Obviously not. If you want to go whore yourself off to the same people who ruined me then go ahead, don't expect my blessing . . . "

« But these are also the same people you're trying to get back in with, aren't they? »

[The Director concedes that this is true.]

" It sounds like a trap. That kid has it in for me after what I did. "

« What did you do? »

" Go read a newspaper sometime. "

« I'm sorry, I know you don't think I monitor your
career, but I do, I monitor it . . . »

" He might have beef with me after he got involved
with *Klopp*. There were rumours that he, because he
was so young and not intended as an actor . . . that he
might've been traumatised by the burning of Klopp at
the end of the movie. They say he's a dangerous
psychopath these days. "

« You burned Clop? »

" Oh relax Isabella, he was a fuckin' immitant. "

« There are studies that show immitants can feel
pain . . . »

[The Director feels anger and balls his fists so tightly
the blood could very well rupture his knuckles.]

" This conversation is officially over. "

[In the street outside a car has swerved and crashed
into a hydrant sending a plume of water from its gate
valve. The water smashes down onto the car bonnet
where a red orchid of blood turns everything ugly.]

■

(*At former child actor* ~~Stanley's~~ *place*)

« Isabella! Come in! »

[Isabella is amazed to find that the person answering the door isn't an eight-year-old boy, but an adult, a tall, good looking male in his early 20's with wide-flung shoulders. Isabella can't stop thinking about how betrayed the Director would feel if he found out she was here. She enters the apartment and takes a seat on a tatty leather sofa. The floor is covered in various ornaments of crap . . .

In the music of a bleak silence, ~~Stanley~~ pirouettes between obstacles of furniture, sidestepping trash as he goes.]

« Care for a drink? » [he asks. Isabella kindly refuses.]

[He sounds tender and non-threatening. She becomes distracted when he pulls free a packet of rubber medical gloves from somewhere in the kitchenette. He starts slapping them on, massaging his wrists and palms with lubricating oil.]

« Don't worry, I won't be a minute. »

[Then he disappears through the back behind a tarp. Isabella can hear the grunts of an animal. ~~Stanley~~ leads in a large domestic sow from behind the curtain barn by a leash of worn rope. It looks happy enough. The pig is clapping the hooves of its trotters, nestling itself into a comfortable sitting position. Isabella can tell straight away that the pig is well trained. ~~Stanley~~

drags through a wooden trough brimming with wet food and the pig swabs its tusks hungrily preparing to stuff itself with the contents of the ravine.]

« Nice pig . . . »

« Thanks. »

« I'm really looking forward to working with you . . . »

« Yeah, me too, me too . . . »

[When he resurfaces he's holding a large apparatus that Isabella initially worries might be a hand gun—

No.

In ~~Stanley's~~ hands is a bolt pistol used to execute livestock. He tells Isabella this while cocking it towards her playfully. The hard black phallic barrel molded from steel alloy supports itself by rubber washers and a mushroom tip. Isabella knows what the device does. She's even a little aroused by the shooter until she becomes conscious of how the boy intends to use it on his pig. He places the weapon on the animals forehead and fires a blank cartridge of compressed air through its cerebellum that exits out its gullet. A spray of blood and matter wash over Isabella's horrified face. ~~Stanley~~, unfazed by the quantity of blood covering him, kneels down to deliver the fatal blow. He cuts its neck wide open expunging the pig at once. The pig (*Bessie*) makes one final tortured squeal then thuds to the floor, releasing a reflex yelp from Isabella, who is visibly appalled that the pig has been terminated. A pint of black pudding floods from its neck wound and spills across the floor like water bursting from a leaky valve. Already the place looks like an abattoir. With no pause for breath, ~~Stanley~~ retrieves a large carving knife from a cutlery drawer and begins dismembering the corpse. First he removes the intestines, then amputates the liver, which he tells Isabella he will cook for her when he's done. ~~Stanley~~ says this in such a way that he expects her to be appreciative of his generosity. The pig neck is flapping about as if she were merely a plasticised rubber prop. He asks Isabella to help him cut the animal in half so he can de-bone it, but the girl is frozen and can release only a whimper. ~~Stanley~~ goes about hacking off the pig's head with his knife instead.]

« We can get more trimmings from the meat around Bessie's head. »

[He strains, one arm locking the neck in a vice-grip, one arm tearing away with his surgical blade. Between the crunching of Bessie's dislocating limb bones and the moist slap of her vital organs landing on the metal surface, ~~Stanley~~ is greedily cleaning the blood from his disposable nitrile gloves with his tongue. Isabella can't help but feel this brutal massacre to be wholly unnecessary.

She has never seen a living thing slaughtered before. ~~Stanley~~ is already carving slices from Bessie's rump and tossing a couple of peeled bacon strips with membranes of gristle cartilage onto a sizzling frying pan.]

▸ *Is he trying to impress Isabella with this display? Is he simply warning her of how imbalanced he is? Is it a premeditated demonstration of masculinity?*

[Isabella hugs her knees close to her chest, rocking back and forth in a crunched fetal position. The pig's decapitated head has ceased rolling about, but is now in a position to observe its own body being slung up on meat hooks by ~~Stanley~~ through its unblinking slits.]

« I hope you're not about to tell me you're a fucking vegetarian? »

[He laughs so hard he chokes on his own saliva.]

« Once we eat this I'm going to kill you. » [~~Stanley~~ says this so noncommittally it's almost not threatening. Isabella realises the Director was right all along.]

« You don't look surprised. »

« I'm not. He told me you were fucked up and would try to hurt him somehow. »

« I hear he's a junky now . . . »

« That's correct. »

« I'm glad. D'you know it was my part in his very unique film that made me this way? He abused me as a child. I should never have been part of that. Can you believe they wanted to cast me in a sequel? »

« Isn't it enough that his career is probably completely over? »

« You tell me? Would it be enough for you if he'd ruined your childhood, inflicted such awful images onto your young mind? What if he'd been so callous that he didn't even care about the consequences of his actions? I want to see him burn like Klopp . . . »

« He *has* done all those things to me though. »

« What? »

« I was in his first movie. He actually impregnated me and filmed my abortion. That was all real. He raped me all the time too, off-set and on, he still does. He never paid me for my part in the movie either. He hits me and always ALWAYS condescends to me. He ruined MY childhood and being with him is ruining my adult life . . . »

[Isabella realises the Director needs her more than she needs him. She knows the reality of things—that they are merely bound by a tenuous link . . .]

« Then why the fuck are you with him? »

« Because I love him. »

« Why? »

« Because I'm the sympathetic character, ~~Stanley~~, it's all I know how to be. He fucks me around and I fall deeper in love with him. I can't help it. The Writer dictates what he does now, but the Director has always dictated me, even though I was only ever in one of his movies. I'm his *creation*. Does that make sense? »

« Fuck no! You sound like you're the servile character, not the sympathetic one. »

[In the mirror, she finds herself oddly pleasing which rests her unease if only in a superficial way. Isabella has noticed how every mirror reinterprets her physical features differently. It's almost as if the mirror was only designed to complete a silent function, adjusting and touching up the onlookers imperfections and returning pleasant white lies of observation. Mirrors lie, probably why magicians use them to manipulate their audience.

Pores of early morning puncture from behind the dead pig. This drab light gathering in the corners o the room cover most aspects of ~~Stanley's~~ portrait.

Isabella is directed to a store cupboard. She tries to dash past ~~Stanley,~~ but he is much too strong, forcing her back into the room. Isabella is bundled into the cupboard as though she were a suitcase being stored away for winter. The boiler room next to her hisses.]

■

(In the producer's penthouse somewhere. His name is Ivan Boulder)

[Mordecai and his right-hand man Casper (an immitant of one Casper Layman) stare down at the blubbering producer. He sits on a toilet bowl fenced in by a wooden cubicle. There's a piece of graffiti Casper finds particularly amusing—a large erect penis with three drops of semen dribbling from the tip, above which an illiterate attack on someone named *Davie* has been scrawled. Puddles of urine have gathered all over the rotted lino. The producer is in a right old state. His head fizzes and his ears are singing from repeated blows. Though both lackeys are bearing down on the producer, at first glance, he is a terrifying presence himself—with a hard cube for a skull, like an old bust-up Skoda dropped into a car crusher.]

« Stop crying, you dumb cunt. »

[The producer is bald and has both trouser legs of his bloody orange overall sucked into a pair of insulated socks.]

« Big boss isn't happy with you. He hates crying little girls too so just, yano, give it a rest. »

[The Writer enters.]

« Boss, this is the producer. His name is Ivan Boulder, or it used to be . . . »

Boulder? [the boss scoffs,] **of the New Hampshire Boulder's?**

[Gerard and Casper laugh on queue.]

You've been rumbled, Ivan . . .

[Derek listens from outside the bathroom door. The people in the restaurant are none the wiser. Derek is glad his dad finally trusts him with something. He hopes he'll get to watch the slaying of Ommensetter next. This is a real master-class of writing—an author going above and beyond to fix a mess he's made. He takes some notes. He goes back to listening.]

You can't be trusted, Ivan my old pal.

« Don't kill me! »

[The Writer gives a fierce cackle.]

Jesus, Ivan boy, we're not gonna kill ya!

[Ivan, the producer, gives an audible sigh of relief.]

We're gonna have to make sure you don't talk though . . . Casper, if you will.

[Casper lunges at him with a pair of pliers and begins yanking at Ivan's tongue until it tears free in a gob of dark blood and saliva. Derek only hears the scream.

He knows what they're doing. Big boss looks happy
then suddenly unsatisfied.]

**Gotta make sure you don't try and write anything
down either . . . Casper . . .**

[The crony ducks into the cubicle again and begins
clipping each of the producer's fingers off. Derek
shudders. He isn't really into this side of the ugly
writing lark.

The boss turns the tap on and washes the blood from
his hands. He tightens the spigot and signals for
Casper and Mordecai to follow.

The boss turns to Derek and, with an expression that
almost dawns on pride, says,] **You done good . . . for
a faggot who can't write.**

[Derek beams.

So buoyant in his paternal acceptance, he pirouettes,
and then his dad tells him to **Cut that shit out**. From
the bathroom Ivan the producer yelps from his
tongue-less mouth. Derek puts Ivan's pain to the back
of his mind and follows his dad and the two cronies
outside to the limo. Mordecai holds the door open for
the Boss to get in but blatantly denies Derek the same
courtesy.]

« Open the door yourself . . . »

Be nice to the boy, he done good. Cut him a little slack.

[Derek gets in beside his father. Casper looks at Derek and sees how uncorrupted he is. Casper feels like he has to explain to the boy how he got to be such a nasty customer.]

« Listen kid-o, I used to be an evil cunt, not now. I was frustrated, being an immitant. When I found out I went off the rails. I used to get off to the whole crony business, editing folk out of existence. Couldn't hack it now though, I'm a changed man. I just believe in good films and good writing. Your dad here is the best. When I was young it was all stupidity, didn't even seem real. Was like a fuckin' video game or something. The respect, the power, the money, the bitches, it was the fuckin' high life. Not now though, priorities are different now. I just do what I'm told, go home and wait till the Writer needs me again. He rewrote my whole life, man, and I couldn't be more grateful. »

[The Writer butts in.]

At least you got a dad. My dad stepped in front of a bus when I was eleven years old. I loved my dad. They said when the train hit him he burst like a bag of meat. Found bits of him all over town. Found his wedding ring finger in a thorn bush. I bet there are bits of him scattered all over the

Slave State still. You couldn't write that kind of hilarious tragedy . . .

« I still want to kill the original Casper Layman. Then I could die a happy immitant. »

Be patient and do a good job, then I'll grant you the ending you desire so much . . .

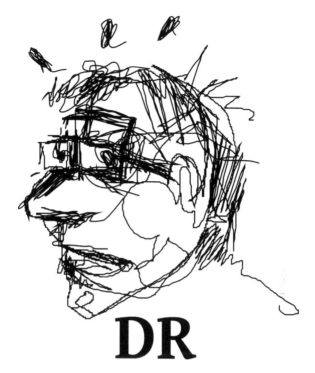

DR

KRICFALUSI

ONE

(*Panoramic shot of a busy Spokane airport. Baggage handlers are smoking cigarettes on their lunch break, businessmen and weary families eye the departure boards anxiously while waiting to board a delayed flight. Mr Kricfalusi stumbles out of the toilet. The left side of his head has been shaved bare and a Nazi swastika has been etched across his face in black ink. His shirt is untucked and his tie has done a 180 over his shoulder. He appears dazed, injured. There are several cuts and bruises over Mr Kricfalusi's face and body.*)

(*Kricfalusi stumbles towards a customer service agent who is busy typing on a keyboard.*)

KRICFALUSI → Yes, I'd like to report a crime.

CSA → Okay sir (*CSA looks up from computer screen with a shocked expression.*)

KRICFALUSI → You see, a gang of teenagers just attacked me, shaved my head and painted a Nazi swastika on my face.

CSA → Yes, I . . . can see that . . .

(*A flight attendant stares gawk-eyed at Mr Kricfalusi. Other people start to notice his appearance. A woman gasps off-shot.*)

KRICFALUSI → I'm on my way to Bucharest. I don't want anyone on the plane to get the wrong idea about me. I'm not a Nazi. The pen won't wash off, I've tried. They must've used permanent ink or---------------------- ---------------

(*We see that the attendant is pushing the ALARM button repeatedly under the table.*)

KRICFALUSI → Sir . . . could you perhaps issue an announcement to the passengers on my plane so they know I'm coming and that I'm not some insane fascist?

(*Two security guards appear either side of Mr Kricfalusi. They lift him up by the armpits and lead him off in the opposite direction.*)

TWO

(A customs officer is sitting at his desk staring angrily at Kricfalusi. He has a dishevelled handlebar moustache and top teeth that look like a row of derelict council flats.)

CO → Do you think this is funny? I suppose you think this is pretty funny?

KRICFALUSI → No, this isn't funny!

CO → We don't want any trouble here, I suppose it's trouble you're after here?

KRICFALUSI → No! I just want to report the crime and catch my flight to Bucharest.

KRICFALUSI → Bucharest? It'll be a Nazi convention you plan on attending I assume? Can I assume that? A Romanian Nazi sympathiser convention, or some such, am I correct? Disorder and anti-Semitism no doubt? We don't tolerate Anti-Semitism in Spokane, no we do not. I suppose it's hate and anti-Semitism you plan on breeding? You can't have thought you'd get away with this, surely you couldn't have thought that? It's our responsibility to make sure people like you don't leave the country, you know? Did you know that?

KRICFALUSI → I'm not a Nazi! I was attacked and vandalised by hooligans!

CO → And who would do that to you? More to the point, *why* would someone do that to you? Hmm? Liberals, eh, liberals who disagree with your fascist attitudes I suppose? A maniac sir, you are a Nazi . . .

KRICFALUSI → I'm *not* a Nazi! I just need to get to Bucharest for some cleansing powder and alcohol to sterilise my operating utensils!

CO→ Wait, *you're* a doctor?

(Kricfalusi looks puzzled.)

KRICFALUSI → No . . .

FIVE

(Back at Isabella's apartment, the Writer pays a visit)

[The Director opens the door and sees a familiar face—it's Klopp. He takes a step back into the apartment and leans against the sofa in shock. Klopp enters and music follows. His hair is a glistening spectra of colour.]

" *Klopp—?* But, you're dead? "

No, I'm not dead, and my name's not Klopp. I'm the Writer.

[He clicks his fingers and the music stops. The Director thinks that he's come to offer him a deal, a deal that would see him welcomed back into Hollywood. The Writer enters the apartment.]

So how are things going since your banishment?

" If you're the Writer then you'll know already. "

[The Writer turns around and grins.]

" Klopp is based on your image? "

He is an immitant I had made especially for that purpose, yes.

" You're that self-obsessed? " [The Director tries to make this sound like a jape but it comes out petty and confrontational, as if the cock had said it instead.]

I'm obsessed with myself in some ways, yes. I'm obsessed with suicide.

" Suicide? Really? That's fascinating. "

It isn't. I enjoyed the final scene where Klopp is burnt alive. It made me feel like I was watching my own gruesome death. Don't tell me you've never fantasised about that?

" Maybe on a slow day . . . "

[The Writer laughs.]

" So, what brings you to the hole of the Zinc Theatre? "

Yes, I'll get to that . . .

[The Writer observes the apartment and tuts at its tasteless décor.]

Ugly room, ugly, ugly, ugly.

{ *I send death letters to famous writers. I told one writer that his excremental book made me kill my wife. This isn't true, as I've never actually been married, but I wanted to let this author know that his book was so awful that it drove me into a fit of homicidal rage. My akashic knowledge of art in all its mediums means I am best qualified to pass judgement.* }

You know, I was once an operator in a screening room for erotic movies way back when. At work one morning, I'm in the projection booth and something strange happens. There came a crying from inside the cinema. Three seats down. It was a feminine kind of sob, the kind you might hear in a downtown bathhouse. On screen a man was having his buttocks kneaded in a sauna room by a fragile little Islamic catamite. The sobs were muffled, there was effort being had to hide the guy's grief. I could really only make out muted sniffs. Just when it seemed like his torment was over he explodes into a full blown wailing.

" How bizarre. "

Bizarre is right. The guy on screen was a big chap, Mexican or Puerto Rican with a crotched moustache. The little Turkish kid worked up his

inner thigh, rubbing oil towards the money shot.
During the glazing process, the man three seats
down starts wiping mucus trails onto his sleeve.

Wonder what was wrong with the guy three seats
down?

His crying had become disruptive and annoying.

Did he find his homosexuality morally
reprehensible?

Surely all those tears can't just be for violating
that first amendment?

Hmm . . .

Mewling for the mother he never told he loved,
who stroked his hair and rubbed his back and fed
him from a repository of tartan-patterned biscuit
tins?

Wanker . . .

Maybe the father he neglected to please? Or all the
other people with whom his life was once made
complete? He has been raised, taught, loved and
cast in an image with all the expectations that
accompany such a design. His failure to adhere
will have been met with the unanimous disgust of
his relatives. For years I'd been rolling these films

for fags and hetero's alike, but I've never seen one break down here before.

" That's a strange one. "

The blue movie hits its erotic peak when that big mammal turns over and presents unto the cabana boy his penis, golden and margined by dark pubic hair. A splatter of semen fountains at the screen. This elicits further wailing . . .

" May I ask, what's the point to this story? "

The point is . . . Polly cries and Patrick cries.

" Meaning? "

Meaning you're pleasing no one with your masturbation, your procrastination. Your time at the Zinc Theatre is almost up.

" Then what? What if I don't do a damn thing and I want to remain an outcast? "

You'll go to the worst parts of the Slave State. You'll be the first person in the entertainment to be entirely banished from this realm.

" I tried so hard with *Klopp*. "

There's an old poem that goes . . .

[~~The Writer clears his throat. The reader groans and wonders why he/she is still reading~~]

THE BOY WHO BROKE HIS BACK
AND FLUFFED HIS LINES

NEVER BEEN TOO GOOD

A RAW NERVE COLLISION

EXPLANATIONS DIZZY ON THE TONGUES ROLL

BUT . . .

PEREMPTORY MOTIONS

PALM FACING TO SHUN THE LIGHT

ON THE BACK

KNUCKLES TORN, RIVETTED

'NEVER TRUST A MAN WITH A SMALL NOSE'

FRAIL TOPMOST DIMENSIONS

PALADIN? NEVER!

EYES SHINING LIKE BARNACLES

THE DALE OF MY GROIN

PEOPLE ARE HUSHED

SPICE OF MULLED WINE

LOOK AT ALL THOSE EMPTY, INDIGNANT DISHES

GRINDING NAUSEA

THROUGH THE STRICTURES OF AN HOURGLASS

HOLD THE SMOKE IN

SUCK MY TEETH

BONES PICKED CLEAN

TRYING TO TWIST

BREAK MY BACK

You know who wrote that?

" Who? "

ME!

[The Writer approaches the Director.]

You don't get to make decisions, you only think you do. What you did to my screenplay is

unforgivable, but Mordecai was insistent that you were up to the job. I mean, your background is as an artist for fuck sake! Boy was he wrong! You took ALL the fun out of that picture and tried to be an auteur. Well guess what, that's not your fuckin' job!

" Are you going to kill me? "

No. You've got a much worse fate in store. *Time is a teacher,* and all that . . .

■

(A dingy strip club in downtown Wire City)

[The Director ducks under the frame of the door carrying with him a musk of outdoor Zinc Theatre. The club is dingy and the feeling of the Writer's omnipresence leaves him paranoid. A pole dancer conceals the mallows of her substantial breasts. The Director's glassblower nose rises into the air, inhaling the syrupy fragrance of perfume. Lurking in the crook of the bar he observes another girl dancing inside a booth. He finds her routine alluring, pleasantly distracting. The girl folds around the pole as if she were boneless, allowing ochre threads of hair to dangle into a flame while she stretches her neck beyond her back. The girl has kept the same performance going since she started at the club, a performance that has gained her a dedicated following. The Director can tell the girl is popular. Once her bare breasts have been unleashed in all their glory her admirers are sent into rapture. A salvo of green notes are tossed at the glass cage which the barman collects into a small metal lunchbox. Under the thump of electronic rhythms, the owner introduces the next dancer and the girl finishes her frolic with a curtsey. The Director sees where he went wrong all this time. Art should've never come into this whole nasty business. THIS is what the people want.]

" I loved a girl once. She didn't love me back. You love what you love, not what loves you. "

[The Director feels the cold hand of death on his shoulder . . .]

HERE . . .

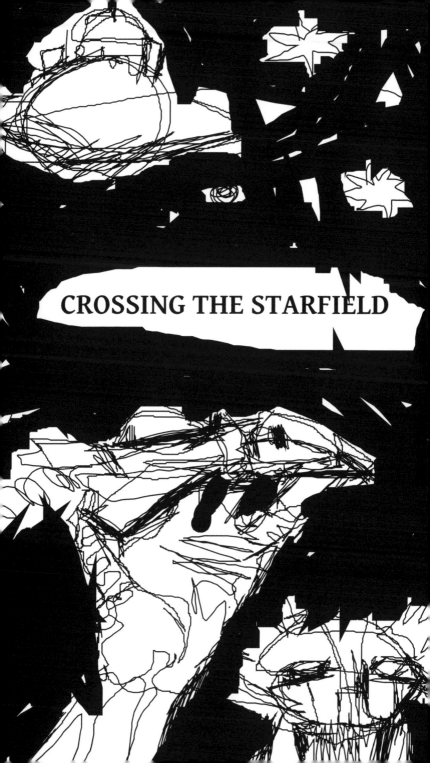

CROSSING THE STARFIELD

1

(Black screen—A voice declares in sepulchral tones that the planet's economiser is overheated and in need of immediate maintenance. The two girls stargazing on the tundra snow bank ignore the plea. Tilly and Eve are obviously lovers. Fade-in . . .)

TILLY → D'you ever wonder what it might be like as an Outsider?

(Tilly asks while gently stroking her own forearm.)

EVE → Doesn't bear thinking about.

TILLY→ Aren't you ever curious exactly what Outsiders do all day?

EVE → I imagine it's completely awful. Sit on their backsides and twiddle knobs till it's time to clock off, bureaucrats the lot of them!

(Tilly and Eve stare at the reflective two-way wall of the tundra's dome. The reinforced globe separating Outsiders from Insiders is impenetrable—unless someone expresses a desire to switch sides. This happens, not often, but it does happen. These people are referred to as 'Swapers'.)

(Insiders can become tired of the grim reality of an observer, of progress charts and endless CCTV monitoring, locked up in a planetarium all day long; similarly Outsiders occasionally grow weary of their life of ignorance, seclusion and servitude.)

*To switch sides is a frightfully complicated process. It involves submitting CV's to Uppers, if you are accepted you're then summoned to government quarters for assessment. Even then transference is far from guaranteed. Individuals must cross the Starfield—a mental test created by Uppers to ensure that the natural instincts of a Swaper can cope and adapt with the change in climate and lifestyle. This is the phenomenon Tilly is experiencing currently. She has an urge to see the Outside.

TILLY → I've been thinking about transference you know.

EVE → Forget it, no one gets out, not ever. I'm bored of all this talk anyway, I thought you had something else in mind bringing me out here.

(*Tilly notes the tone of disappointment in Eve's voice. Seeking to remedy this, the girl undresses. Eve's frown becomes a wide, full-toothed smile.*)

(*A pinhead of moonlight shines through the dome, but the white desert seems to remain untouched by it. Eve looks up at the maze of cables and pipes traversing the surface of the ceiling as she approaches a climax. The jagged edge of Tilly's pelvic blade digs in sharply with each thrust. Eve's body, black as shale, writhes under the feline figure of Tilly—an overhanging Krummholz covered in permafrost sets a webbed shadow over the girls' naked twinning. When it's over, they stay locked in the Lotus position.*)

2

(Tilly and Eve lie in the snow bed, shucked behind a slice of sheet metal forming around them like the shell of an oyster or a clam. Light penetrates the sloe eyes of young Tilly.

She has to see what's out there . . .

The Upper headquarters are barely visible in the distance, but the Penrose triangle of the company's insignia can even be seen from the Insider dome; their company motto—'There ain't no such thing as a free lunch!'—emboldened just below it.)

3

(Scene opens on a heated argument—Tilly can hardly meet her father's (KAL) eye. The notion of one of Kal's children converting to a 'Swaper' is utterly unthinkable.)

KAL → There are two types of people in this universe, Tilly: Outsiders and Insiders. Now you were born in the tundra to near seven generations of Insiders, it suits us in here. We live simple lives, prepare for ice harvests and provide other planets with sustenance and thermal energy. We don't belong out there pushing buttons and observing.

(Kal is a massive man, a true product of the Insider way of life. His forearms are as thick as two planks of plywood and his skin is eroded in callused whorls. He is a proud man and proud to be separated from the awful Outside.)

TILLY → But father, transference is common.

KAL → Common? Amongst whom? I've never known anyone to switch allegiances . . .

TILLY → You make it sound like we're at war! It does happen, Father

KAL → Nonsense and bullshit, now it's time you got back to work at the accumulator tower, the solar collector is running low.

TILLY → Father, I have submitted a CV and it's been accepted . . .

(KAL slams a meaty fist against the closed vessel of a cryogen chamber.)

KAL → No one gets out, not ever! My great, great, great grandfather was one of the first men on the tundra when it was terraformed. Doesn't that mean anything to you?

(It didn't . . .)

4

TILLY → I can't believe you're leaving . . .

*Eve is emotionless but enjoys drama and generating sympathy. Tilly plays along.

TILLY → It's something I have to do.

EVE → But you don't *have* to do anything.

TILLY → Why should I stay?

EVE → What about me? Isn't that a reason?

TILLY → Come with me.

EVE → No.

*Tilly is secretly relieved but feels compelled to ask why.

EVE → I like it here. Couldn't you consult with another Swaper? Someone who's come from the Outside to the tundra? Find out what it's like from them? See if it's worth it?

TILLY → No.

(The girls embrace before Tilly lopes along the bridge to the departure pod heading for the Uppers HQ—then eventually on to the Starfield.)

5

(*Tilly secures her harness as the pod disengages from its port. She finds herself next to a bald man with severe features. He appears nervous as the pod burners fire to life. Tilly glimpses out the aperture as she is jettisoned from the tundra dome and into the stratosphere.*)

The shuttle ride is a bumpy one, the cast iron walls rattling over the pod's noisy engine. Tilly has a look around at the other handful of passengers, all men. She tries to communicate with the nervous skinhead next to her, whom she vaguely recognises as Chet the molten salt technician.)

TILLY → Chet, is it?

(*The bald man stares at her out the corner of his eye distrustfully. He doesn't reply, only ups the collar of his coat and buries his mouth under it. The Penrose triangle inches closer.*)

6

(*The vast matrix of space is an overwhelming sight. From inside the dome the distance between Insiders and Outsider had seemed only glass-thick to Tilly, but the pod has been in orbit for almost 2 hours, and there is still a way to go.*)

(*Chet has dozed off, emitting a low inhaled growl followed by a whistling nasally exhale. Tilly looks over her CV and feels happy with it.*)

(*Suddenly, an almighty jolt rocks the vessel, waking Chet from his deep slumber. Tilly becomes anxious. A voice comes over the intercom, not unlike the expressionless orator who declares news of faulty economisers back on the tundra.*)

TANNOY → *There has been a technical problem. Please tighten your safety harnesses. We are approximately 200 miles from Upper headquarters*

(Tilly sits back in her seat and tries to remain calm. These efforts are almost ruined by the gibbering mess cowering next to her. It seems Chet has lost his nerve.)

TILLY → Are you alright?

CHET → I know what the problem is . . .

TILLY → You do?

* Tilly's expression is sceptical—suggesting she finds it surprising that a molten salt worker could have any grasp of the mechanics of this complex ship.

CHET → It's Lobo . . .

TILLY → Lobo?

CHET → The creature who stalks the Starfield.

(Tilly is unaware of any such creature. She has studied the process of transference with intricate detail—it seems implausible that something like this could've been omitted from her learning.)

EVE → There's no creature on the Starfield. It's a government made region specifically designed for the mental and physical assessment of potential Swapers like us, not an ecosystem for bloody space monsters.

(Chet is unconvinced. He peers out the aperture as if he half expects to see the beast hunched on the shuttle's wing. Tilly

tightens her harness and tries to ignore the delusional
skinhead.)

(Another jolt sends the pod careening to the left. All passengers on the starboard side go crashing into the opposite end.
Two large men land hard against Tilly, tearing her free of her
harness. Tilly and the two brutes squash against the wall of
the tilted vessel. To Tilly's horror, outside the window she
sees a massive claw clutching the underside of the ship, like a
small child observing a replica schooner in an empty beer
bottle. The mighty talons on its hideous, spider-like fingers
are lodged with rods of bones and the concaves of partially
smashed humanoid skulls. Tilly can't believe her eyes. Other
passengers soon notice the creature. Its head rises slowly into
view.)

∎

(CLOSE UP ON LOBO'S FACE—The creature has two flashbulb
eyes that reflect the stricken expressions of the ship's
travellers. It must be around 50 feet tall with bubbling boils
covering the surface of its hide. A pug nose steams up the
aperture with noxious breath as the voice emerges over the
intercom once again.)

TANNOY → *We ask that all passengers try and
remain seated during this turbulent environment*

(The voice sounds fraught with dire portents. Chet is clambering towards the cock pit, hurdling a maze of broken seats, a pistol clasped in his hand. Tilly becomes more concerned by the increasingly manic behaviour of Chet than Lobo outside. The ship rocks back and forth as the creature tries to shake out its contents. Suddenly the shuttle breaks in half at the centre.)

(Tilly sees a dozen or so passengers descend into the oceanic abyss below. The sound of slowly creaking metal is awful, the screaming more so. Trapped in one corner of the split vessel, Tilly is now confronted with the beast. She hears Chet's pistol fire once before an oblong shape tumbles over the edge of the craft and into Lobo's cavernous maw. While his original prophecy seemed outlandish, Chet's demise was hardly unforeseeable. Blackness engulfs everything and everyone. At first it's difficult to tell if the cabin lights have ceased or if she's been cast out into the infinite realms of space . . . then Tilly realises she's been swallowed.

The girl slides down the slime-strewn oesophagus until she lands in an effervescing, acidic reservoir of stomach fluid. Tilly chokes on the in-surge of pungent gut nectar until she finds the pool to be only a foot deep. To her surprise the acid hasn't melted her flesh to bone and she steps safely onto an embankment. The inner sanctums are honeycombed with rounded ridges of similar curvature to the gentle slope in Eve's thigh.)

(She wonders if this is part of the Upper's assessment.)

SANDEEP → Hello . . . *(Spoken barely above a whisper.)*

(A woman, Punjab descended, is standing in a red sari, staring at Tilly.)

TILLY → Um . . . hello . . .

(The woman motions toward Tilly—she can sense no threat from her.)

SANDEEP → I am Sandeep. Welcome.

TILLY → Welcome? I don't understand?

(Sandeep has a warm, kind expression of perpetual understanding. She takes Tilly's hand in her own.)

SANDEEP → You have stumbled upon our colony. Follow me . . .

(Confused, Tilly follows Sandeep through the fleshy gastrointestinal bowls of Lobo.)

7

*(The women travel in silence for almost half an hour.
Suddenly the distant flickering of torchlight burns through
the cavernous tunnel. Tilly sees the commune sharpen from a
blurry mirage to a portrait of jagged building contours.)*

*(Sandeep takes Tilly to a large monastery with windows of
shattered stain glass images. A banner reading "COMPLETE
INGRATIATION" dangles across the steeple. Inside, the corpse
of a large tentacled creature has been skewered by an
inverted crucifix at the vanguard. A teardrop of viscera
bleeds from the creature and collects into a wooden bowl.)*

TILLY → This is your church?

SANDEEP → Please do not be sceptical. This is
Interfaith.

TILLY → Interfaith?

SANDEEP → We are a sanctuary for people of all denominations. Whether you believe in the Hearth or Snub Nigguraath here *(Sandeep gestures towards the sacrificed octopod),* whether you're Muslim or Gnostic, you are welcome in our place of worship.

TILLY → I just wanted to cross the Starfield . . .

SANDEEP → The Starfield?

TILLY → I'm an Insider. I want to be an Outsider.

SANDEEP → Tilly, you are beyond the Outside realm of Uppers and Swapers, Inside and Out, simply beyond it!

(A reptilian-looking male wearing a scuffed leather jacket and a cowl walks to Snub Nigguraath's pronged carcass, glares for a moment, scrunches up his face in an illustration of disgust then hawks up a wad of sputum before gobbing it over the octopus. No one is shaken by the incident, people barely acknowledge the outburst. Noticing Tilly's yearning for an explanation of some kind, Sandeep explains that the two creatures were once enemies. The reptilian man is considered a diabolist—*and, as Sandeep keeps reminding everyone, that's okay here too.)*

8

(Tilly and Chet are standing in a red, sodium-lit hallway.)

TILLY → You made it down here too, I see.

(Tilly is amazed to see Chet, alive and seemingly full of renewed vitality. He's inclined on a hut with his name scribed on the wood in red ink in what looks suspiciously like his own blood.)

TILLY → Chet, I thought you killed yourself? I thought you were dead?

CHET → Hell, even I thought I was a goner! But hey-ho here I am . . .

TILLY → You seem perkier.

CHET → Well why the heck shouldn't I be? I finally got what I always wanted. Eternal life, away from the tundra confines!

(Chet's skin looks patched together. He's sweating profusely and there's a frailty about him that was absent before, like he's suffering from a chronic bout of Botulism.)

TILLY → What d'you mean eternal life?

CHET → Hell, this demon's belly is purgatory or somethin', cos flesh doesn't rot down here. It has these sustaining properties, holy properties that sort of put pause on your living decomposition. Nobody ages or gets sick, it's great! I don't know why I was so afraid of big ol' Lobo, he's the best thing that ever happened to me!

(Chet doesn't appear to be quite himself.)

TILLY → You've settled in quick.

CHET → Quick? I been here for days.

(Tilly's confusion mounts.)

TILLY → The creature literally *just* swallowed you . . .

CHET → Don't think so, I'm now a converted Yahweh Methodist, Jew Fundamentalist.

(The girl leans against the spongy membrane of the monsters gut. She rubs her cheeks and tries to make sense of everything.)

TILLY → But . . . you know there's no Christian god. You've lived in a terraformed snow-globe your entire life, you know there's nothing out there . . .

CHET → That's just it, we don't know. We've been prisoners our entire lives!

TILLY → And we're prisoners again.

CHET → Only this time, we don't have any option! So I suggest you pick a faith to invest your energy in and try complete ingratiation. No one gets out, not ever.

TILLY → Christ, Chet . . .

CHET → Can I ask you, who do you think put us in that snow globe?

(Tilly can't dignify the question with an answer.)

CHET → I believe in what I choose. Interfaith allows me this freedom.

TILLY → If you were going to worship anything, you'd think it would be Lobo himself. After all, it's because he consumed you that you're here now. That's fairly godlike wouldn't you say?

(Chet gives a pitied laugh, rubbing the nut of bone at his knuckles absent-mindedly. Tilly turns to leave when he calls her back.)

CHET → Why did you leave the tundra? If you're not happy here, maybe you just can't be happy anywhere.

(Tilly thinks about this and her face becomes pained. Fade-out . . .)

9

(Fade-in—Tilly is making her way back down the darkened passage leading to the Interfaith church. She scans the peripheral surroundings with disdain—the pink columns of ooze, the pools of bowl content, the jagged, ugly architecture, the community politics and flourishing madness of it all . . . she could never settle here . . .

It seems the only option for the hopeless girl is to end her life. Having exchanged one snow globe for another, these are clearly the cards the great cosmos have dealt her—destiny. There is no escape from destiny. Tilly's mind wanders to Eve and the notion that she may have actually loved her.)

(Sandeep appears beside her.)

SANDEEP → You said you wanted to cross the Starfield, Tilly. In exactly ten mega-parsecs you will have achieved that goal.

TILLY → How?

SANDEEP → Lobo courses the divide between tundra and Upper HQ. In ten mega-parsecs he will pass the Starfield terrain.

TILLY → That's not the same.

SANDEEP → You mean you *wanted* the assessment?

TILLY → I just wanted out . . .

SANDEEP → No one gets out, not ever. Stay, Tilly. I know your mind has gone to a dark, desperate place but you must resist the desire to unburden yourself.

(*In the distance, a cabal of Harry Krishna's chant the Maha mantra.)*

SANDEEP → Remember, you cannot run away from life here. Killing yourself won't work.

(*An anchor of nausea sinks in Tilly's stomach. She drops to her knees and looks up into the shadowy ceiling of Lobo. She feels like begging, but has no idea who to plea to. Suddenly an intercom pops—a voice declares in sepulchral tones.)*

(A stagehand comes on holding a board that reads—"No one gets out, not ever".)

SIX

(In ~~Stanley's~~ cupboard)

[Isabella can hear a conversation through the wall.]

« *This isn't working out, Blair, I don't think it's working . . .* »

« *Um . . . 'it's not working out'? Um . . . what? I mean . . . ?* »

« *Yeah, you know, I just think that, like, it's not really . . .
that's to say, like, a relationship isn't really what I want
right now, you know what I mean or . . . ?* »

« *Um . . . okay . . . so, what, this is over now?* »

« *Yeah, I think it is.* »

« *Okay, great, cool, Laura . . .* »

« *Yeah . . .* »

[*Blair gets up to leave then stops and looks at Laura.*]

« *Can I just ask you, like, one thing?* »

[*Laura nods while getting up and stuffing her purse into her handbag.*]

« *What changed?* »

« *What changed?* »

« *Yes, what changed? Is it the way I look or is it, like, my personality or something?* »

« *Why would you even want me to go into this?* »

« *Because I want to know. It's called closure and I want to know.* »

« *Listen, I care about you and I know how sensitive you are, so if we could just both go off in the opposite direction that'd be great for me . . .* »

« *Um . . . no. I don't really give a shit what would be great for YOU, because YOU just ended this and YOU don't get to decide these things. You already dumped me so you already have all the power, I'm just asking for this one thing. I need closure, now come on . . .* »

[Isabella has been in this cupboard for what feels like hours. She's stubbed her big toe on the hinged door panel during an attempt to escape. Furthermore, uncertain of what ~~Stanley~~ will do to her when he returns, she has lost three acrylic finger nails trying

to slip some part of herself under the ventilation stile.
The stench of Bessie's body clenches her stomach
tight. She's now sure that rumbling away in the boiler
room next to her is some kind of propane-fuelled
incinerator. A heat from the cremator's furnace in-
tensifies her sense of despair. Isabella has realised
she's so frightened and firm with fear that her voice
has forgotten how to use itself. Choking a whimper
she seeks to accept the inevitability of her demise,
reflecting over a life barely half-lived. The pulley
conveyor belt creaks away between two pipe flanges,
spinning heavily like an iron giant stirring in a scrap
yard. Isabella thinks about being oxidized, about her
bones burning to an urn's worth of ash. Suddenly, the
crash door swings open outside, followed by footsteps
clapping up the landing stairs. Small glimmers of
light hop around under the door's slit.]

■

(*In the Writer's bank of raw, partially repressed memory, a*
boy's stark realisation about the world . . .

In the distance a sleek limo drifts along the country-road
dirt track. Cars don't come by this town too often. You have
to drive through country paths to get here. It descends
silently, like a shark weaving down to the ocean's basin. The
road leading in had once been an old corpse road, now
Death is returning disguised by a hearse. Between black-

eyed skies cracking above meadows and the over-polished fuselage of the limousine, the town is presented with an arrival of something altogether sinister.

An off-duty policeman with ducktailing chin straps stands beside a fuel pump filling his car with gasoline. He's wearing a plane white t-shirt tucked into pre-shrunk jeans. The policeman takes one look at the oncoming limo then plugs his fuel cap.

The Writer is taking cover in the long grass from his friends. His breathing has become heavy. What began as a seemingly harmless game of hide-and-seek quickly grew more serious as the children's imaginations began running amok. The vast expanse of farmland presented the kids with some unique hiding spots.

The limo enters the town square and slows down as the Writer pops up from the meadow. He walks towards the car. A good looking man, like a young Brando, appears behind the lowering veil.)

« *"Awright, wee man. Fancy going a run?"* »

« *"I'm not supposed to . . ."* »

« *"What's your name, wee man?"* »

« *"Can't tell you that . . . "* »

[*The man gives a hoarse laugh.*]

« *"Yer a clever boy . . . "* »

« *"Yup . . . "* »

[*The limo driver starts the engine back up. The young Brando takes a sip from a cocktail glass before addressing the Writer again.*]

« *"Before you know it pal, no-one's gonnae listen tae what you've got to say."* »

« *"My mother will."* »

« *"Naw son, even she won't give a shit eventually."* »

« *"How do you know?"* »

[*The Writer flicks his fringe from his face revealing an angry brow. The man takes another sip from his cocktail.*]

« *"Yer mum ever give you in trouble for anything?"* »

« *"Well . . . sure . . ."* »

« *"Well wait till you've made your first **big** mistake. It's awe doon hill fae there son. Before ye ken it, she'll be dead."* »

[*The limo drives off and the Writer never sees or hears from the young Brando again . . .*]

(*Back in ~~Stanley's~~ apartment*)

[Isabella knows he's outside. She knows he's coming. ~~Stanley~~ has returned to finish the job. Under the door stile, that dancing ebb of light has ceased and now occupies the dark shadow of *his* static silhouette. But instead of the cupboard door flying open and ~~Stanley~~ lugging the girl into the cremator, Isabella continues to sit in blackness. There's a squeaking of rubber being handled, a crackle of Styrofoam curry boxes collapsing onto ~~Stanley's~~ damp wool carpet, a clattering of crockery but no disclosure of the man himself. She sits in the cupboard like Gauguin's vision of human misery—the Grape Harvest in Arles. Then the cremator rumbles into life. The door unlocks and Isabella struggles to prepare. *Click, Click, Creak, Creak.* A flush of daylight pours into the enclosed space. ~~Stanley~~ positioned before her, panting, encouraged by the girls tremulousness, his nose frescoed damson by cold snap. Isabella stands to attention.

~~Stanley's~~ fist is clutching the handle of a paper bag that's seeping from the inside through polythene. Noticing Isabella's interest in the bag, he reaches into it to present her with the contents. His fingers are a Turkish tile blue brought about by bad circulation.

There's the <u>Director's head</u>, cropped at the jugular, presenting an expression smooth as glycerin. Isabella's howl escapes like the accented rasp of a barred owl that's flown into the wheel of a bench grinder.

« Say hi, dear. » [~~Stanley~~ places the head to his ear making out as if the Director is whispering a reply. Suddenly he plugs back the barrel of a gun that he frees from his belt. Jerking open the cylinder, ~~Stanley~~ places a single bullet inside to complete a set of fully loaded chambers.]

« Are you afraid right now? I'm going to kill you because you're a poorly formed stereotype. You're not real, you'll never be half the actor I was. I was a REAL actor. »

[Gripping it by the butt, he then places it on a table behind him. He's wearing a backpack. It resembles an aqualung, complete with diving cylinders full of compressed gas. ~~Stanley~~ places a medical mask, attached to the backpack by PVC tubing, over his mouth and turns a valve. After a deep breath of amyl nitrate he coughs a wad of sputum up onto his wrist. He goes to curse the Writer under his breath then thinks better of it.]

« They say a human being's mental capabilities are limited by an inadequate blood supply. Removing certain parts of the brain isn't nearly as barbaric as it may seem to someone as stupid as you. »

[~~Stanley~~ grins once then seizes Isabella.

Pigeons are cooing oblivious outside. The sound of a door being thrown open is followed by the grousing din of the cremator machine. This machine isn't just any old run-of-the-mill kiln. It's an authentic, scaled-down version of a 1941 coke-fired Topf, double muffled, incinerator furnace used by German Nazi's in Auschwitz. While being burned alive would be a real drag for just about anyone, to Isabella, (her Wikipedia page states that she's a descendent of Dutch Jews who arrived in the Moosejaw over 300 years ago as furriers which, of course, is impossible), this slow, painful death would be significantly unpleasant as her heritage forbids by Halakah that the *soul* experience this kind of pain.

Isabella sees Jewish torture in ~~Stanley's~~ eyes too, some private Holocaust that might go some way toward explaining his instability. A terrifying observation— ~~Stanley~~, the *Sonderkommando* putting one of his own to death.

Almost in now . . .

The furnace spits ember and comets of coal from its flaming mouth, grazing against the side of the girl's face. With ~~Stanley's~~ hands wrapped around Isabella's wrists he reverses her into the burner.

Almost, almost . . .

« You stay back! » [A threat that convinces no one of her authority. The girl is trying really hard. She thinks about her body entering the machine oven, her remains travelling down a chamotte grid, collecting in a channel then being scraped away into a bite-size wrapper to be consumed by ~~Stanley~~. As emaciated as the bean-pole boy appears he is incredibly strong.]

« You people think you're destined for an afterlife of interminable ecstasy? »

[~~Stanley~~ is grinding his hands around the slender tubes of Isabella's wrists, inflicting Chinese burns on her flesh.]

« Your moments of clarity are nothing but tricks of your own perception. Tipping your heads back, staring at clouds, you see shapes and believe yourself to be engaging deep into spheres of self-actualisation, when all that's really happening is severe hypotension caused by the rush of blood spilling to the back of your skull. »

[~~Stanley's~~ monologue appears to be a rehearsed one, probably recited many times before this and written with the sole means of devaluing esotericism.

His dry, mummified skin becomes transparent to the hard bones underneath.

Almost in now.

Isabella can hear Donovan's "Colours" through the thin panels on the wall.]

"*Yellow is the colour of ma true love's hair, in the morning, when we rise . . .* "

[The pacifying beauty of the Scottish chanter seems to have a profound effect on both girl and her oppressor.]

"*Blue is the colour of the sky-ay-ay, in the morning, when we rise . . .* "

[The girl seems to have gained strength from the music while ~~Stanley~~ has reacted with the opposite effect. Isabella has started to fight back and with success.]

"Green is the colour of the sparkling corn, in the morning, when we rise . . . "

[~~Stanley~~ is the one facing the furnace now. The boy, for the first time, displays signs of unease, a distressed cadence indicative of how unexpected this shift in power is to him. Then—a tangle of hands and wrists and legs, a girl's fingers wiring inside a wet, warm mouth, then a push in the chest, a fist in the eye socket, a squish like an anvil on gastropods, an *almost* toppling giant, a labyrinth of bodies twisting, the panting and puffing of struggle, a decagonal of nails descending, scratching like tacks, tearing away, making rough skin wet with blood, he's almost in the cremator . . .

The music cuts for a minute before starting back up again. There is a divorce in the natural speed of time for a second where Isabella looks into ~~Stanley's~~ eyes and sees that she has won. Reaching for the gun the girl fires off two rounds that strike ~~Stanley~~ in the belly, sending him catapulting backwards at great speed. As if by an intricate synchronicity Donovan's song resumes.]

"Mellow is the feeling that I get, when I see her, mm hmm, when I see her, uh huh. That's the time, that's the time, I love the best."

[He's finally in the boiler. Every lanky inch of the
villainous male gobbled up by intense flame.]

*"Freedom is a word I rarely use without thinking, mm
hmm ... "*

[Isabella slides the gun into her belt. Then there was
Bessie the pig—gutted, decapitated and diced into
cloves for a fatty brunch. Isabella is lying on a heap on
the floor. Having succumbed ~~Stanley~~ to the cremator,
she takes a load off. His feet are still poking out of the
furnace's mouth, shuddering only in the occasional
spasmodic reflex. Slowly his patent leather balmorals
are inducted by the fire, smouldering through the
sole ... then the flesh ... then the metatarsus and
then finally the insole.

Isabella lives. Somewhere the Director cries, filled
with loss and regret.]

WHO WAS

GLEN OMMENSETTER?

Poverty of Desire

[He was once an artist. Barely a week after arriving in mainland France, Glen Ommensetter was arrested and extradited to Wandsworth prison for sprinkling the royal ashes of a recently deceased French monarch on his porridge (as part of an artistic response to a newly imposed taxation on immigrant residents). He saw out four years of a seven-year sentence.

While inside, between sculpting marble phalluses and creating canvases of smeared faeces, Glen dreamt of returning to the city from which he hailed. However, he was denied entry to his homeland in Glasgow on the grounds of moral turpitude.

Glen fled Earth on a departure pod. He highlighted Mylar 5 as a preferred destination—Glen's installations were particularly well sought after there.

■

Glen somehow got Bellona, an ammunitianist's wife, back to his duplex apartment on Mylar. Bellona was a typical product of the planet—sallow skinned with papery eyelids, boxy jaw, and stacks of muscle bulging through her liturgical garments. He wooed her with the finest wines in the galaxy, told her that her eyes shone like the emerald moonlets of Terra and listened intently to her inane stories about aspirations of monkhood and her unshakably austere religious belief in the Hearth. Bellona was beginning to show signs of weakness. It was time for Glen Ommensetter to make his move.]

" I want to have anal sex with you, Bellona, " [he proposed casually between stoops of radioactive yellow wine. The girl looked surprised but not horrified.]

« We do not do *that* here, » [she said matter-of-factly.]

" You are missing out on so much. "

« By anal sex, you mean . . . » [Bellona gave a Southerly gesture with her eyes,] « in the place of excrement? »

" Come now, beauty is inextricable from grotes-query . . . "

« No . . . » [Bellona seemed mildly offended now.]

" Why do the people of this planet deny their own anuses? "

« You are a victim . . . »

" I am? "

« The poverty of desire is too evident in your eyes. »

[Ommensetter could feel his opportunity slip away.]

" I've gotten this far. "

« You are obscene. »

" Well, I have always been a prostitute, Bellona. Perhaps one day I'll direct pornography? I'm always looking for a leading lady . . . "

[The girl stood up as if to leave. She upped her hood and told Glen she better be on her way. It had been days since he last experienced intimacy, and that was in the company of Night Slime. He yearned for something more formal, more passionate and resonant, something to inspire the art in him—anal sex with the ammunitianist's wife was the only way to appease his starving desires.]

" Please, I'll do anything— " [Glen was aware of his pleading tone. The girl was as intrigued by the artist's submissiveness as she was by his lust.]

« Very well. Since you simply *must* have me . . . we shall organise coitus . . . in the place of excrement . . . »

[Glen could barely contain his joy.]

" Oh Bellona, you will not regret this! "

« There is a catch . . . »

[Bellona shrugged off her vestments. She stood before Ommensetter, bare-breasted and fully nude, save for a peculiar device wrapped around her thighs. It was metallic with a triple-pronged plug outlet at the centre.]

« My husband the ammunitianist does not trust me while he is away, so he had me fitted for this garter belt. Only he has the plug to remove it. »

[Glen could've screamed.]

" So how the fuck are we supposed to fornicate? "

« If we go into the city centre, there is a plug maker I am acquainted with who could get a replica made . . . »

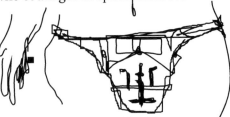

[In the descending elevator, Ommensetter blankly surveyed the city that whizzed by either side of him. The pros outweighed the cons in this situation, that was plain for anyone to see, but he never subscribed to the theory that desire is the root of all suffering. He had to get Bellona into bed.

At the agreed destination, Glen bought a coffee—Earth replicated. He broke two tabs of sweetener into the thick foam. This was frowned upon, to publicly consume the foods of your native planet. Visitors to

Mylar were expected to ingratiate themselves completely, adopt the local habits and pray every day to the Hearth—that went for everyone, even famous, respected artists. People were watching him scornfully as he drank quietly in the sidewalk bistro—but Ommensetter prided himself on the image he'd created, he was untrammelled by any convention of the times, no matter what planet he was on. He was, even then, an auteur.

A hooded monk sat across from him, just glaring. His face was shrouded in shadow except for the lit tip of a Mylarian tobacco cylinder. Ommensetter knew immediately this was the plug maker.

The monk stood up, tamped out his tobacco cylinder and made his way to Glen's table.]

« You are a fool to drink that here. »

" It's really rather tasty. "

« Taste has nothing to do with it. »

" Are you the plug-making chap? "

« Yes. »

" Wonderful, we can dispense with formal chit-chat then ... "

« Typical human. »

" I'm obnoxious even for an Earthling, my friend. "

« Yes . . . well, I can help you in your adultery. »

" Splendid. "

« Do you have the outline of the outlet? »

" Ah yes— " [Ommensetter pulled out a detailed blueprint and a clay impression of the insert holes.]

« A Dimerian, interesting . . . »

" Can you replicate it? "

« Of course. It'll take time though. »

" I'll give you three hours. "

« Very well . . . The poor ammunitianist is keenly aware of his wife's infidelity. A Dimerian lock is very expensive. »

" Can I ask you something? "

[The plug maker nodded.]

" If you're so holy, why are you helping me bonk a wealthy, married Mylar woman? "

« Everyone has a price. Madam Bellona indulges certain needs of my own. Plus, I'm something of a clairvoyant. I've seen what happens to you in the end. You'll end up without a head. The Slave State awaits you . . . »

[This confused Glen, but his insatiable lust for Bellona's dark places quickly banished this nagging doubt.]

« I have never been a fan of your work, Glen
Ommensetter. »

" Oh really? I honestly couldn't give a damn. "

« May I ask from where you originally hail? »

" I told you, Earth . . . "

« I mean which region? »

" Glasgow? "

« The City of Cages? »

" The very same. "

« I have heard awful thing about that region. »

" They're probably exaggerated, I mean look how well I
turned out. "

[The plug maker raised his eyebrow unconvinced.]

" Now, if you'll excuse me. I look forward to hearing
from you again in exactly three hours. Contact me
through Bellona. "

∎

[Back at his sealed, airless conapt, Ommensetter
looked for Bellona. She promised to stay here until he

returned. He called her name but received no reply.
He saw a trail of orange alien viscera leading from the
walkway into the bedroom. Glen prepared for the
worst. He ran a hand through his thick greasy mop of
hair, every part of himself clenched. The corner of the
bedroom entry had smudged handprints of orange
that dragged at the fingertips. Sure enough, there she
was ...]

" What are you *doing?* " [demanded Ommensetter.]

[Bellona seemed surprised to see him. The girl was
covered with Mylarian blood. A figure lay motionless
and crumpled underneath the ruined Moroccan bed
sheets.]

« Did you get the plug maker? »

[Slowly, Glen moved towards the chastity-belted girl
sitting nearly naked on his bed.]

" Yes, yes I found him ... what are you ... ? "

« I had a vision. »

" A vision? "

« Yes, my duties are manifold. »

" What is it with you Mylarians? You're all fucking
mental! "

« He was the stigmatist. »

" Who was? " [Ommensetter was at the bed's edge now, trying to see who/what slaughtered creature was underneath the covers.]

« Do you still want to penetrate me? »

" Well . . . " [Glen felt bad to admit it, but he really did.]

« Come . . . »

[Bellona extended her hand for Ommensetter to take, which he did. They then writhed around on top of the wasted corpse. Bellona's garter belt fell off, hitting the wooden tiles with a dense *schunk* sound.]

" But I thought . . . "

« I told you, I've had a vision. I have seen the stigmatist. »

[Bellona grabbed at Ommensetter's genitals. She squeezed it tightly in her fist until her thumb and finger tips met around the engorged helmet. The cock spoke for the first time; it said ▶**YES**◼. The second thing it would say, incidentally, was ▶**Go to Hollywood**◼. Glen's eyes were awash with white static, he was having a vision of his own.]

" The Hearth . . . " [he said . . .]

« Yes, you see . . . »

[Bellona worked her hands along the base of the artist's penis. He began sweating, stiff to the point of light headedness.]

" Yes ... "

« You see ... »

" I see my next work of art ... the tender mercies of a
psychopath ... "

[Glen surged in a borscht of hot jism which pumped
over Bellona's clenched fist. The Hearth, along with
Glen's artistic inspiration, was gone.]

« You saw ... » [Bellona kept saying, still massaging
the flaccid flesh in her hands.]

" No, " [said Glen, to Bellona's obvious disappointment.] " The ammunitianist can have you. "

[He turned to see a figure in the doorway—a man
holding a plug fixture, chord dangling.]

■

[Ommensetter left the apartment right away. He had
prepared a departure pod to Terra 5, the oil planet. A
sudden desperation overwhelmed him, a new kind of
desperation. In that singular hand job, Ommensetter
had been drained of all his artistic inclinations. He felt
it. Something had stolen it from his soul. Now he was
on his way to Terra to hold down a modest riggers job.

Glen Ommensetter thought about Glasgow. The cold, harshness of the city struck him in a way it never had before. A grim reality set up camp in his mind's eye. He felt baron of anything. He fled Mylar knowing he'd left a part of himself behind. A new path penned by another, a career outside of art, the work of a writer's lackey, but the voice of creativity would not be silenced forever.

It would be a long time till he craved the flesh of an adult woman . . .]

NO ONE

■

{ *In Tuscany I started these memoirs and only when I re-verted to past recollections from childhood did everything suddenly discern itself. I learned that to be a good writer you had to call upon what you knew best. Unfortunately I had had no real experiences (I rarely ventured out of my small town, in fact) and I certainly hadn't had any sexual encounters (at twenty-three I was still behaving like a moppet, a naïve stripling). So, in effect, the only thing I ever really "knew" was, well, me. Still, I regrettably cast myself out of the district with no sexual skill to speak of.*

My father was ambitionless. That's not meant to sound undermining or to in any way challenge his obnoxious temerity, it was just his way. I wrote about my hatred for him while travelling Damascus. In retrospect several observations have caused me to revise this hatred.

Before my father died he said he did not, under any circumstances, want me to be a writer. He became aggressive the more I defied his wishes.

I stopped answering back because I knew he was just bored. As the great writer/philosopher Eric Hoffer once claimed— "When people are bored it is primarily with their own selves they are bored." His life was taken up by his stevedore duties and even when his passion died with his youth, a lack of qualifications stuck him to professions of limited skill. One's sense of humour does tend to suffer at the hands of an expanding intellect, perhaps I'd failed to detect his irony.

His family strobilated sequences of bored organisms with short-lived engines, tired from birth. He had me convinced that writing simply wasn't to be my melic. }

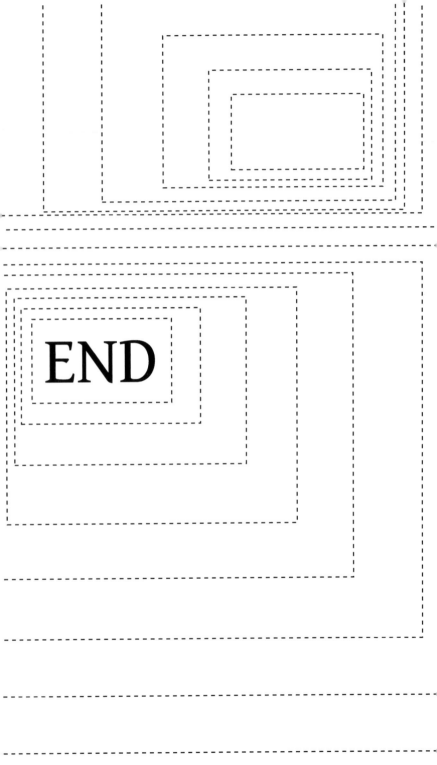

END

ROLAND BAKSHI, a journalist working for Star Parts Magazine, conducting interview with the Director about his upcoming novel: URSA MINOR'S MILES DAVIS APPRECI-ATION SOCIETY. The Director scratches at the cast around his neck.)

DIRECTOR → My book is an exploration of the human being, the triumph of individualism over collectivism. I deny the paternity and refuse to marry the mother . . .

BAKSHI → Um, we haven't started recording yet, Mr Director.

DIRECTOR → I realise that.

BAKSHI → Of course . . .

(Bakshi clicks on the Dictaphone.)

BAKSHI → So Mr Ommensetter, first of all welcome back from the Slave State. Now, would you say your book is an exploration of the human being? Kind of like an illustration of individualism over collectivism? Almost as if you were somehow . . . denying the paternity?

(Bakshi pauses his Dictaphone while the Director replies.)

DIRECTOR → Yes . . . I just said that

BAKSHI → No . . . you didn't.

DIRECTOR → It feels good to be back.

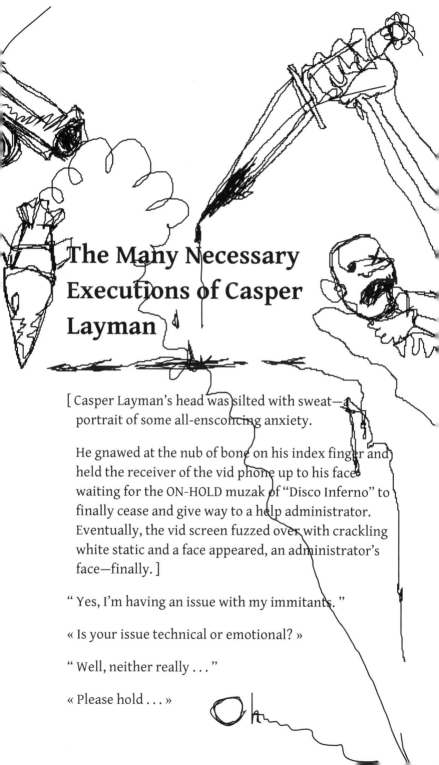

The Many Necessary Executions of Casper Layman

[Casper Layman's head was silted with sweat—a portrait of some all-ensconcing anxiety.

He gnawed at the nub of bone on his index finger and held the receiver of the vid phone up to his face, waiting for the ON-HOLD muzak of "Disco Inferno" to finally cease and give way to a help administrator. Eventually, the vid screen fuzzed over with crackling white static and a face appeared, an administrator's face—finally.]

" Yes, I'm having an issue with my immitants. "

« Is your issue technical or emotional? »

" Well, neither really . . . "

« Please hold . . . »

■

[A doughy face materialised through the nebulous dot-patterned frequency—behind him aseptic tiles were set in alabaster. The administrator seemed morbidly obese slumped in his pivot chair, when he spoke his folds of gullet fat pendulated.]

« My name is Strasser. State your place of origin, » [the grease-bag asked without a hint of feigned courtesy.]

" Ersatz. "

« Galactic coordinates? Please sir, we deal with many problems, not just ones on your godforsaken boondock planet. »

" Longitude: 179° 56' 39.4., latitude: +0° 2' 46.2. "

« Thank you, sir . . . »

[It was eternally dusk in Ersatz, a crepuscular haven of faulty droids and abandoned bistros. Layman had lived here almost his entire life, a quiet, rather impoverished existence.]

« What is the nature of your immitant related problem, ₁ sir? »

" I believe they've been victims of the Japanese crime syndicate. "

« I . . . see . . . »

[Strasser adjusted his buttocks on the pivot chair and clasped his hands together.]

" It started a week ago. My friend in Florissant called me to say one of the immitants I'd commissioned had been murdered, a grizzly end, decapitation . . . "

« I see. »

" I'd had that particular droid in Florissant made to live with an ex-girlfriend I couldn't face breaking up with. "

« Perhaps your ex-girlfriend killed your immitant. »

" No . . . "

« It's not uncommon for an individual to become enraged by such deception, maybe she discovered the immitant wasn't really you and destroyed it in a fit of frustration? »

" No, you don't understand. My ex-girlfriend is a good woman, a little possessive and over-bearing, but generally an innocent enough girl. This droid was decapitated, brutally decapitated . . . "

« That's still not enough, sir . . . »

[Layman scratched the bowl of his shoulder, becoming a little frustrated.]

" I'm not finished. "

« Please, go on . . . »

" I admit the droid in Florissant could easily have been a one-time incident. But then I get a call from another friend in Shell County, my wife in fact. "

« I . . . see . . . »

" She seemed rather shocked when I answered the vid-phone. Of course, that soon gave way to blind fury. It so happens there'd been a burglary and another im-mitant had been strangulated with a piece of piano wire, another decapitation. "

« Hold on a sec—*your wife?* »

" Yes. You see, I missed Erstaz and decided to commis-sion another droid to appease my then-wife Bellona, only Bellona knew she was living with an immitant.

She was perfectly happy with a version of me that cooked and cleaned and didn't talk much. I got a job as an ammunitianist. She was quite pleased from what I hear. "

« Okay . . . »

" THEN, not a day later, I receive a call from the Slave State officials inquiring as to my whereabouts on the third. Apparently a body had been discovered in an alleyway near the Lafayette area, chest exploded from close range gun fire, head resting separately by its side, sewn off with a meat cleaver. "

« That is certainly quite a coincidence, » [Strasser still sounded unconvinced.]

" There's more. The final incident happened just this morning. A drive-by shooting took down my fourth immitant as he sat and ate in a Central West End restaurant with an old college room-mate of mine whom I can no longer stand to be in the same company as. Police say a group of people came back minutes later to remove the head with a garrotte . . . "

« And the Japanese did this? »

" I have five immitants, four of them have ceased to function. "

« Sir . . . »

" It's led me to the conclusion that . . . someone is trying to kill me by process of elimination. "

« Please, sir . . . »

" One murder, that can happen. Two, maybe—but four separate isolated executions of droids in my image? It's beyond coincident, Mr Strasser . . . "

« So you're suggesting? »

" Yakuza or Shell County Triads . . . "

« Why would they be after you? Why would they remove the head every time? »

" No idea. They remove the head because it's the only way to tell if a person is real or an immitant. "

[The door buzzed, startling Layman. He was terrified to answer it.]

" I have to go, " [he told Strasser and cut connection with his help administrator. He got up, unbolted the reinforced lock and peered round the side.

It was . . . Layman! The last immitant.

Layman figured he'd better let himself in, maybe he was on the run. The droid pushed into the apartment, panting, out of breath. When he caught a clean gasp of air, the two Laymans, immitant and original, stood staring at each other. This lasted about three minutes. The enamel on Layman's teeth began to itch in an odd response.

'The Uncanny Valley', they called it . . .]

« I didn't know where else to turn, » [the immitant tried to explain.]

[Layman noticed his immitant wearing a rather expensive, if scuffed, leather jacket. He also noticed a miasma of alcohol surrounding the edgy droid.]

" Have you been drinking? "

« It was a natural, impulsive reaction to the situation. Even though I cannot experience the dizzying heights of inebriation, it somehow felt . . . necessary. »

[The immitant's eyes had a cold brilliance which was unsettling. Layman invited the droid in and they both sat on opposite sides of the trestle table positioned at the centre of the kitchenette.]

" Do you want another drink? "

« No, thank you. »

" I trust you've heard about the fates of your contemporaries? "

« Yes. It's only a matter of time till I'm next. »

" Who's doing this? "

« I don't know. I keep dreaming of the same cardboard city. »

" Cardboard city? "

« Yes, strewn with shadow. »

" Do you think it's significant? "

« The immitant in Jefferson County recollected a similar recurring dream, we corresponded briefly. It could be a sign of imminent non-functionality, oblivion. »

[Layman was overcome by a sudden revelation. He too had had that very same dream. Not anytime recently, but it had happened. It sounded joltingly familiar. The immitant picked up on the affected template of his designer's expression.]

« Are you alright? »

[Layman was muted by a sudden influx of doubt. He's
   heard that immitant prototypes often shared dream
   content and synchronised brain activity. He became
   wary, paranoid. The droid had picked up on the
   change in atmosphere.]

« Unconscious wish fulfilment maybe? »

" I had that same dream . . . walking through the
   thrown ramparts of a destroyed city of soggy, wilting
   cardboard . . . the ruins beneath my feet . . . the awful,
   consuming shadow and sense of dread . . . "

« Perhaps we're more alike than you think . . . »

[Layman looked up and saw that he was staring down
   the nozzle of a laser cannon directed right at him.]

" You wouldn't dare— "

[The immitant arced his mouth into a grin. The film of
   artificial flesh stretched obscenely at each corner of
   its mouth. A ribbon of daybreak shone through the
   Venetian blinds of Layman's conapt in piercing
   pinpricks of light. An embossed letter sat on the
   trestle table, envelope slit open at the seal.

« I finally got you, Layman, you dirty bastard. [The
   immitant kept grinning.]

" I don't understand . . . "

« I've lived the sad, pathetic life of a coward for too
long, Layman. It's time for a change. God made man in
his own image—I suppose that makes Layman God? »

[Layman kept his eyes fixed on the laser. His mirror
image kept talking.]

" « I want to be something more than a man who can't
face his own problems . . . can you understand
that? » "

[Layman didn't admit it, but he understood.]

" « Once you have an immitant made, you can't recall it.
Having five of you made was the biggest mistake of
my life. I want to tackle my problems head on, face up
to them, bite the bullet, be a man about things . . . » "

[Layman raised the gun and tightened his palm around
the butt until the Kevlar material left indentations on
his skin.]

" « I hope you understand, I've worked hard for this
ending, done unspeakable things to achieve it. Even
though you're just a droid, this hasn't been
easy . . . » "

[A laugh in the ocean of sadness . . .]

In the seminar Ali notices Davie is still affected by something. The lecturer points to Davie and asks, "Mr Sock, can you tell me how Ignatius begins undermining business as usual at 'Lexy Pants'? What character makes Burma Jane this novel's eirôn?"

Davie still looks entranced.

" Mr Sock? Mr Sock?? Mr Oppenheim, is Mr Sock alright? "

" He's fine, sir . . . I think . . . "

Ali nudges his friend hard in the ribs. He snaps to attention.

" Eh? Wah? . . . "

" Mr Sock, could you perhaps attempt to show an interest in this class? "

" Sorry, sir . . . "

" Yes, well . . . "

This seems to be enough for the lecturer who passes the question onto another student. The answer seems to be *'there is nothing outside the text'.* The class ends and everyone gets up to leave at once despite the lecturer's warning beforehand to evacuate the theatre single file and in an orderly fashion.

Billy Grieves is tidying his books into his rucksack. Ali drags Davie over to prove once and for all that the whole fiasco about this book has just been a daft practical joke.

" Grievesy? Hoi, Grievesy? Tell Davie that that dogshit book you recommended was just you trying to be a smart cunt, go on, tell 'em . . . "

" Did you not like the book then? "

" What? Are you kidding? "

" It's a bildungsroman masterpiece . . . "

" It's a pile of shit! " protests Ali. He notices Grievesy doesn't quite seem himself.

" Who recommended this to you exactly? "

" Mr McLeod. "

" The writer-in-residence? "

" Yup. If you have a problem maybe you should take it up with him ... "

There is a poster up with another book by the same author on it. Over the exploding head is a headline:

FREE BOOK/SEX/DRUGS/FUCKED UP STUFF
HAPPENING FOR NO REASON!!!

and in smaller print at the bottom:

students must see Professor McLeod for more information.

" This is offensive to human intelligence as well as the people of Saasawthwa, " Isabella says.

There are still places where Isabella will always have the final word ...

Did you enjoy the book?

We welcome all feedback and queries.
Villipede.com

Printed in Germany
by Amazon Distribution
GmbH, Leipzig